The Best Crew

A Romance Novella

Phebe Powers

Copyright © 2023 Phebe Powers

All rights reserved.

This is a work of fiction. Any resemblance to actual persons, living or dead, or actual events is purely coincidental.

No part of this book may be reproduced in any form or by any electronic or mechanical means, including information storage and retrieval systems, without written permission from the author, except for the use of brief quotations in a book review.

Cover Design by Rafe Goldberg

For Pops.
Good authors, too, who once knew better words...

Chapter 1
Vacationland

"Welcome to Vacationland."

Startled, Sam ceased his absent-minded gazing out the dusty window and glanced in the direction of the driver's seat. "What?"

Kat clarified without taking her eyes off the road. "That's what they call it, the great state of Maine." She inhaled deeply. "Mmmm, salt air and pine trees."

Sam laughed. "I think that's the air freshener you're smelling. Seeing as how the windows are closed."

"Well, let's fix that!" She took one of her hands from the wheel and started to crank. "Sorry, but like the locks and the gears, the windows are manual."

Sam had noticed the little knobs when he'd gotten into the decidedly antique vehicle. He'd also noticed the funny little noise the engine made whenever they switched gears—but Kat swore up and down that Moby Dick, as she called it, its being the appropriate size and color, was fit to drive, and who was he to say otherwise?

Once they'd rolled both of their windows open, Kat switched off the antiquated AC and instead let in the fresh and bracing wind. Sam took a deep lungful of the air coming in and—

"Ohhh, yeah."

"What did I tell you?"

"I hate to say it, but you were right. About both the salt air and the pine trees. I didn't know highways could smell this good." Sam shook his head, impressed, then stuck his face back out the window.

Glancing over at him, Kat laughed. "You look like a golden retriever when you do that."

Obligingly, Sam closed his eyes and let his tongue loll out of his open mouth.

"Put it away, Fido."

Chuckling, he closed his mouth. Then opened it again to ask, "Why *does* this highway smell this good?"

"We took the scenic route. In a bit we'll be pulling into Bath, then over the bridge. I wanted to give you a taste of the coastline before plunging you in headfirst."

"Ah, so we're swimming to Juniper Island?"

Kat barked a laugh. "Please. I bet you won't even be able to dip your toes in for longer than a minute."

Sam grinned. "Challenge accepted. We'll let Will time it."

Will was Kat's brother, and Sam's other best friend. He'd met the Abbott twins at boarding school when they were all just barely fourteen. The three of them had hit it off instantly, their friendship founded on a mutual disdain for the cool kid clique of incoming freshmen who lacked acne and had already figured out how to style their hair.

Bonded together by initial unpopularity, Sam, Will, and Kat were inseparable from the start, and quickly found further common ground: shared taste in good books and bad movies, competitively poor performances in Essex's mandatory two years of Latin, and devotion to a wide range of extracurricular activities—despite achieving a remarkably short tenure at each.

Over the course of their four years at Essex, they were jointly "let go" from the school newspaper, the debate club, the ski club, the ornithology club, and even their own late night radio show, all in record time. Sam was pretty proud of each of these failures, as they represented the mischief that he and his best friends were capable of, when they put their minds to it.

But in all their years of surprisingly serious injuries sustained during pillow fights, sneaking out after curfew to stargaze from the quad, and general tomfoolery that continued into college despite each of them going their separate ways, Sam had somehow never visited the twins at their extended family's shared summer home on Juniper Island in midcoast Maine.

This year, when the invitation came to visit the Abbotts' sprawling compound, long since christened Abbottville, Sam had been determined to accept. And, for once, he was able to do so—in part because he'd recently moved back to Boston after several years in Silicon Valley, granting him greater proximity to the place, and in part because his CEO had given him a little time off before he was supposed to start as her new Director of Analytics. More than a little: a month.

Kat and Will, meanwhile, both had the option of working remotely: Kat as a salesperson for an award-winning cyber security product and Will as a storyboard artist for a small but growing animation company that had recently created an Oscar-nominated short film about onions—a metaphor for emotions, Will had assured Sam when they watched it together in advance of the fruitless awards ceremony.

Will was already on island and had been for the better part of July. According to his last email—apparently texts didn't really go through, on Juniper—he was starting to go stir crazy from the isolation. Not that he'd admitted this. Just something Sam and Kat had surmised.

Speaking of which... "Do you think your brother has actually fallen in love with a ghost?"

Kat laughed. "It's entirely possible, knowing Will. And not a new development. When it comes to this particular ghost... Well, their relationship has always been a bit intense. You weren't there for it last July, but he used to sit on a rock overlooking the thorofare and cry."

Sam furrowed his brow. "Sounds awfully Homeric to me." They had been required to read some of the so-called 'Classics' at Essex. The image of Odysseus, bleaching a rock white with his tears over the course of seven years, had always stuck with Sam. "But why?"

Kat lifted a hand from the steering wheel to wave it dismissively. "Oh, he made some insensitive comment about exorcisms, I think, and she was so distressed, she disappeared for a week before he was able to coax her out of hiding. This year, though, she's gone for good and Will doesn't know why. The planchette didn't so much as move a millimeter, when he finally resorted to the Ouija board." She sighed. "He's still looking for her, even though it's been weeks."

Sam nodded, thoughtfully. "It's hard, when people leave."

After a moment's stilted silence, Kat glanced over at him. "Have you heard anything from Camilla, lately?"

He shook his head firmly, his eyes on a handmade roadside sign boasting of wild blueberries, sold at what he could only assume was a competitive price. "Not since she broke up with me."

Kat nodded in Sam's peripheral vision. "That must have been, what, a month and a half ago?"

"I've stopped counting. Why?"

She shrugged. "No real reason. I just see a lot of her on my Instagram feed. It was Brianna's bachelorette this weekend, apparently. Camilla threw quite the party, according to her story."

Sam shrugged, not exactly eager to rehash the events of June. The break up hadn't been out of the blue. Camilla often complained that his heart wasn't in it, that he couldn't seem to commit. And she wasn't wrong, not really. Sam had cared about Camilla, genuinely. But he hadn't loved her. And that, he feared, might have been an unforgivable thing. To be fair, they'd only dated for six months. And she'd never said them either, those three words she'd apparently longed to hear.

The Best Crew

Sam had never been negligent, or careless, or cruel, but he had lacked passion. Camilla had never inspired it in him. And so he didn't fight for her, when the time came. Not for her, nor for whatever it was that they had had. Because it wasn't enough. Not for Camilla, and not, as he'd come to realize, for him. In many ways, Sam was grateful to his ex-girlfriend for recognizing that while nothing was technically wrong with it, their relationship was nevertheless not quite right.

His elbow out the open window, his legs stretched as far as the broken seat-adjuster would allow, Sam settled deeper into the worn leather and sighed.

Kat eyed him curiously. "Sam? Are you thinking about Camilla?"

No, he was well beyond the break up. More than ready to move on. "What's the population of Juniper Island, again?"

She answered automatically. "Three hundred year round, eight hundred to a thousand in the summer."

"And how long is the ferry ride?"

Again, she rattled the numbers off with that lifelong familiarity. "An hour. It's approximately ten miles."

Sam didn't even have to do the math, although it was easy enough that he could have with a pencil and paper. He just knew that the odds of his finding someone, someone who inspired in him the kind of passion he'd always imagined, on a small island located an hour offshore of midcoast Maine, were not in his favor. Still... "Are there any other ghosts on the compound?"

"Well, there's the ghost in the barn, whom we think is our great great great uncle who died during the Big House Fire of 1910. You know, the one that rendered the East Wing and the West Wing standalone structures. He's a bit of a prankster. And then there's the widow in the woods—she's not one of ours—but I wouldn't mess with her either."

Sam supposed it wouldn't work out, anyway, with an island-bound ghost. Certainly, they couldn't relocate to Boston, much less go out to dinner for date night. How would his companion order? And sex would be pretty solitary. Sam wasn't sure about the properties of ectoplasm, but according to Will, and a certain comedy, when it wasn't intangible it was incredibly messy.

Being a bit messy himself, Sam rather thought he should be looking for someone neat. That was the key to a successful relationship, wasn't it? Balance? In addition to communication, of course, and chemistry. Sam needed to find someone who inspired him, who challenged him—someone who complemented him, more than they complimented him. Someone to whip him into shape, someone whose day he daily wanted to make. And as wonderful as Juniper Island was purported to be, he rather doubted he'd find his ideal partner amongst its tight-knit sliver of a community.

One long ferry ride later, as Kat drove up the winding road that led out of Juniper Island's town and into Abbottville, Sam's heart beat a bit faster with anticipation. From the way her fingers drummed against the steering wheel, he could tell his host felt the same.

"Oh look! There's Will. I hope he hasn't lost any fingers." Kat's brother had set off the miniature cannon to mark their arrival; they'd heard the blast from the ferry as they were coming into the thorofare. Apparently it was a family tradition.

Kat pulled past a pond and onto a lawn that apparently doubled as a parking lot, then turned off the engine. She and Sam both jumped down from the old truck as Will ran down from the small cluster of buildings, and the three of them stumbled into a group hug.

"Sam!" Will beamed as they broke apart. "I'm so glad you could make it."

Sam laughed. "As am I! Thanks again, for the invitation."

Kat waved her hand dismissively, even as Will cried, "Of course! Now, would you like to meet everyone first? Or have a tour of the compound and then meet everyone after?"

Kat jumped in. "Tour first, family when they arrive at the end of the month, ghosts hopefully never. The only *living* family member on island is Granddad, but he's always napping. Oh, and Valerie. But she's down at the docks, teaching. And she definitely doesn't have a speech prepared in protest of the fact that neither of us has married Sam yet."

Sam chuckled. "I thought your parents gave that up years ago."

"Yes, but the rest of the family are still holding out hope that one of us will settle down soon, and they're sure to like you when they do arrive. They're matchmakers, all of them, and they'll jump at any excuse for a Juniper Island wedding!"

Kat shuddered. "Enough, baby brother. Let's show Sam around."

Will nodded, then turned to gesture behind him. "That's the East Wing, where we stay. It used to be haunted by the most marvelous ghost…" Will trailed off, sounding sad and wistful.

Kat patted her brother on the shoulder and picked up his slack. "And over there's the West Wing, which is our grandfather's place. It's been renovated for accessibility's sake, plus they recently added an extension for his nurse to live in."

Sam nodded. "What's this?" He pointed to a rickety old building down the hill from the West Wing, with huge closed doors.

Will perked up. "That's the barn! It's haunted, too."

"Right, Kat was telling me. Your great great great uncle?"

"We think. He certainly has the Abbott nose. And then, if you look toward town, you'll see the farm house, and the attached bunkroom, and the vegetable garden! Our Aunt Melissa and her husband, Adam, are in charge of all that. But, like Kat said, they're off island."

Sam was struggling to keep track of all this information, and suspected he ought to have been taking notes. Still, he'd have a month to learn it all, he supposed. "And these all look out over the water?"

Kat nodded. "There's a family dock and a boathouse, both leading into the thorofare. Grab your bag and we'll show you the view."

Will led the way up the old stone steps, past the flower garden, and onto the grassy hill. "We're standing where the big house was, a hundred years ago, before it burned down." He pointed away from town, past the East Wing. "And then, last but not least, there's the Cliff House. It's through Widow's Woods and overlooks the water, as well."

"Who lives there?"

"Our aforementioned second cousin, Valerie. Well, the rest of the year she's in Brookline. And at the moment, as Kat said, she's at work." Will gestured towards the sea. Way out in the middle of the thorofare, beyond the cluster of occupied moorings, there was a small fleet of—

"What kind of boat is that?"

Kat answered with uncharacteristic warmth. "Those are Optis."

"What?"

"Optimists!" Will smiled. "Isn't it sweet?"

"They're like floating bathtubs with a sail," Kat explained fondly. "Easy, safe, small—perfect for children."

"And how does this relate to your third cousin?"

"Second," Will corrected him. "And just listen!"

Faintly, Sam could hear a woman shouting. "Jessica, do *not* t-bone your brother's boat! Marcus, *don't* let go of the tiller. And definitely don't pick up that sponge, or I swear—Oh, come on, you guys. This is not the time to play sponge-tag!" And then, with a surprisingly audible and unsurprisingly exasperated sigh, "James, a little help over here?"

Her commanding tone, as well as the sound of something splashing and children shrieking, carried across the otherwise calm waters of the thorofare and up the sloping front lawn of the Abbott compound.

Sam grinned. "She sounds like she's got her hands full."

His eyes on the far away scene, Will nodded. "Probably literally."

Kat smirked. "She's more than capable of handling a little minor maritime horseplay. Besides, sponge-tag is nothing compared to the games we used to play."

"Oh?" Sam turned to face his friend. "Do tell."

Kat shook her head wistfully. "A couple years back, just after Valerie was promoted to head racing instructor, they did a complete overhaul of the sailing program. These days, it's run by trained professionals. But back when we were kids, we were taught by the teenagers who had just graduated the program. Untrained, unlicensed, unsupervised."

"That sounds... unwise," Sam suggested.

Kat's eyes took on a wicked light. "But not unfun."

Will smiled dreamily. "We used to pirate other boats, for no reason. And instructors would strand students on the nuns."

"The nuns?"

"Those big metal buoy things," Kat clarified. "Some of them ring, like giant bells on the water."

"And they would just... leave you out there?"

"If you were annoying."

"Ah, so you must have been marooned most regularly."

Kat laughed, but Will nodded vehemently. "Kathryn holds the record!"

"The point is, things have changed. Although, Valerie was always pretty straight-laced."

Will shook his head, forlornly. "Wouldn't even let us corrupt her with a rum and tonic, not until she was seventeen."

"She's tough, though," Kat assured Sam. "Not a softie. And she likes her privacy. I'd stay away from the Cliff House, if I were you."

"James!" Valerie shook her head. "Stop mooning over your girlfriend and go help Amelia pull that boat up."

Honestly, James was next to useless like this. Her coworker and friend was a changed man ever since he'd met Estie, the romance novelist who was currently blowing kisses from the back of a passing motorboat. Valerie had had a hand in reuniting them after they'd foolishly allowed themselves to be separated, the summer before. And she definitely didn't regret it, but… people were different, when they were in love. Not that she herself would know, never having fallen into amor's abyss.

James frowned, squinting up at Valerie from the float below. "I wasn't mooning," he replied over the sound of teenagers chatting while they derigged. "As you can see, my shorts remain fastened at the waist."

Valerie rolled her eyes. "Not that kind of—Oh, whatever. Just go help Amelia before she trips and falls into the water." The fifteen year old was currently attempting to pull a 420 hull up onto the float by herself, which was possible, but inadvisable—or at least unnecessary.

Down on the float, James did as he was told. Together, he and Amelia hauled the two-person fiberglass sailboat up onto the dock and into its designated slot. Valerie scanned the rest of the lower dock, surveying her class as they continued to noisily derig their own boats—pulling down jibs and mainsails and rolling them up, securing halyards and removing rudders, wringing the water out of their racing gloves and leaving their boots to dry in the sun that shone down on the far side of the system of floats.

It was a beautiful, bustling day. The Opti kids had been a bit raucous, but nothing she hadn't seen before, nothing she couldn't handle. And the afternoon class, the advanced students who were old enough—who, more importantly, weighed enough—to manage the sailing program's fleet of 420s, had been fairly focused during their team racing drills. There hadn't been any collisions, at the very least.

In pairs, Valerie's students wrapped up on the floats. Their lifejackets either unzipped or discarded and their cheeks pink where they'd forgotten to reapply sunblock, they made their way back up to the part of the dock that had been designated as a teaching area.

The Best Crew

Valerie stood by the whiteboard that dangled from the side of the club house, marker in hand, and prepared to deliver her last lecture of the week.

"As you all know," she announced, watching them settle into their stackable plastic seats, "tomorrow is Friday and therefore your day off."

A couple of brave students cheered, but most had the sense to at least appear disappointed.

"However," she continued, uncapping the marker, "tomorrow is *also* the William Abbott Ensign Regatta. A regatta, named for my great grandfather, that has been held without fail every year for the past forty years. And I hope to see some, if not all, of you out on the water."

Some heads nodded, and several of her more enthusiastic students exchanged eager grins.

"Whether that be in race committee capacity—and I just want to take this moment to thank Amelia, David, and Elena for volunteering to do race committee; I know we're understaffed but you'll just have to make it work—or as skippers and crew in your own right. Certainly, you've all been practicing enough to have a shot at winning that cup."

Valerie had turned to the whiteboard and was starting to sketch the course for tomorrow's race when one of her students muttered, "Not if *you're* racing, cap." The remark was almost lost beneath the marker's squeak. Almost.

Valerie turned back to face the class, scanning the semi-circle for the student who had spoken. "Thank you for that compliment, Jackson. But that's the beauty of sailing: you never know who's going to win. There are so many decisions to make, so many variables to factor in—be it the length of the spinnaker run, the condition of your sails, an unexpected pocket of wind, or the proximity of the moon—what matters most is that you pay attention, and that you adapt. That's what you're here to learn, far more than how to backwind your jib or fly out on the trap—how to be flexible, fleet-footed, *fast*."

Phebe Powers

There was a murmur of agreement, and Valerie resumed sketching, circling the marks and adding an arrow at the top of the board that demarcated the direction of the wind. "Now, I want you all to look at this map. Who here can tell me what point of sail we'd ideally be starting in, if that's the line and the windward mark is there?"

It was an easy question, quickly answered by one of her more popular students. When David supplied "close-reach" Valerie could practically hear several of the girls in the class sigh. She wasn't entirely sure why they were so impressed, given that it was a throwaway, intended to warm them all up before she subjected them to the truly tricky questions about trapezes and tides. But, she supposed, such was young love.

Valerie didn't know much about it, beyond what she read in books. After the awakening that had been discovering her father in the arms of a woman who wasn't her mother, when Valerie was just seventeen, followed up by her finding out that this wasn't even close to the first time Jack Harding had betrayed his wife, love just lost its luster. At least, in reality. In theory—in fiction, specifically—Valerie was a diehard fan. She was an avid reader of romance novels and mourned the golden age of rom-coms like the rest.

But she had no time for love in real life, not when an HEA wasn't guaranteed. No patience for fumbling first dates, no hunger for sex with anyone else but herself, and no desire to eventually inflict upon some poor sucker her disaster of a family. Well, her second cousins were alright. More than alright. But it didn't matter. Because Valerie wouldn't be making any introductions, anytime soon.

Maybe when she returned to the suburbs of Boston, in a month, she'd allow her online profiles to resume. Maybe. Regardless, right now, she was in Maine-mode. After all, August was high sailing season. Valerie had a cup to win tomorrow and a series to dominate over the course of the next four weekends. She couldn't let love, or lust, get in her way. Not that either was likely on this island, surrounded as she was by relatives and students. The very idea of her finding someone, much less falling for them, was laughable. And that was just fine. Valerie was just fine.

Scanning her students' sunburnt faces, she narrowed her eyes. "Alright. You seem to have a good grasp on the art of the trap. Moving on, then… It's quiz time. Roughly, and raise your hands, when is tomorrow's high tide?"

Chapter 2
The Regatta

Valerie was doing more than just fine—Valerie was winning. She surveyed the Ensign's two sails for luffing, a sign that they'd been let too far out and weren't properly catching the wind. The smaller sail at the front of the boat flapped slightly near the forestay. Valerie called out to her crew, who was sitting on the side of the boat, one hand on the upper shroud. "Courtney, that jib needs trimming."

The other woman nodded and began to pull in the jib sheet. "On it. Oh, look! It's your great uncle."

Valerie took her eyes off the horizon for a moment, glancing back over her shoulder to squint in the direction Courtney was pointing. "Uncle Willie?"

Her crew nodded as she secured the jib sheet in the jam cleat. "Yeah, he's sitting in the back of the Woosters' boat. Mac must be driving." Mac had been the Woosters' boat boy for the past two summers; the rest of the year, he was a student at the Maritime Academy on the mainland.

Valerie huffed a laugh. "Well, it's not Uncle Willie at the wheel." Her great uncle, although really he was more of a surrogate grandfather to her, since her own grandparents had died before she was born, had developed dementia several years ago. His decline had been slow but steady, cognitive and physical. It was painful, watching the man who'd helped raise her unravel. But Valerie refused to look away. She loved him too much to let him fade into forgetfulness, not without a fight. Even if she knew, for the first time in her life, it was a fight she couldn't win.

Still, she had her sailing. Uncle Willie had taught her everything she knew, and in return, now that she could no longer be his crew, Valerie was determined to win every race for him. Especially this one, the final race in the regatta named for his namesake. She hadn't won the second race in the set of three, and as a result was tied with Sarah Doherty, who had managed to steal her lead at the last second and pull off the penultimate contest. Well, that wouldn't be happening again.

"We're coming round the nun in a minute," Courtney called out over the whistling wind. "Are you all set to fly the spinnaker?"

Valerie nodded as she prepared to loose the mainsheet from the mechanical winch that was holding it in place. "We'll switch as soon as we've jibed."

"You were always better on the winches than I," Courtney said with a smile.

"It's not a competition, Court."

Her crew snorted. "It's always a competition with you, Valerie."

Valerie pulled the tiller towards her, initiating the jibe. "Watch your head!"

Courtney ducked, easing the one jib sheet loose, while pulling in the other. The jib began to switch sides. Valerie, meanwhile, was busy letting the mainsheet off the winch, which allowed the mainsail to swing suddenly, brought over by the wind and weighed down by the metal boom, to the other side of the boat.

The switch took seconds, and soon the flurry of activity had ceased. Another day, another successful jibe. No injuries, no lost time. "Alright, let's do this."

Courtney nodded, securing the jib sheet once more. She reached for the tiller, which Valerie let go of as soon as her crew had a stable grip. They switched places on the bench, and Valerie ducked down to pull the spinnaker bag out of the locker.

"Everything as it should be?" Courtney asked, glancing down into the cockpit.

Valerie nodded as she retrieved the carefully organized bundle of lines and the expertly folded nylon sail. "I repacked it before we rigged up."

Courtney laughed, shaking her head. "You are a nut."

Valerie straightened, and set to work. "I'm a sailor. A little insanity comes with the territory."

Courtney's response was drowned out by the sound of familiar laughter.

"Court?" Valerie spared a glance in the direction of the stern, her hands still moving. "Was that my—Oh, *shit!*"

Another boat was gaining on them, fast. Too fast. They'd caught a puff just past the nun, it seemed. And they were on a collision course with Courtney and Valerie.

Immediately, Valerie started yelling at them to head up. But the skipper of the other boat, a man she didn't recognize, wasn't paying attention. He was laughing, at something his crew had said. His crew, her cousins. Christ, this must be their houseguest. What were they thinking, letting him take the tiller? "Kat! Will! Watch where you're going! This isn't some fucking pleasure cruise!"

Kat whipped around. "Oh! Hey, Valerie!" Her face fell as she assessed the situation. "Shit. Sam, you've got to steer us away from that boat!"

But it was too late. If they were close enough for Valerie to hear their conversation, over the wind and the waves and her heart's racing, they weren't far enough away to avoid hitting Valerie's boat. Unless…

"Courtney! Pull the tiller toward you."

She stared at Valerie. "But we'll jibe again, and the spinnaker's half-set—"

The Best Crew

"Courtney, *pull the tiller toward you.*"

Ever her loyal crew, Courtney did as she was told, yanking hard on the tiller even as Valerie rushed to prepare for the jibe. "Valerie, duck!"

But Valerie was already down, having unclipped the aluminum spinnaker pole just in time to pull it down into the cockpit with her. Once the boom had passed overhead, she straightened. They were still on the verge of a collision with her cousins' Ensign. "Court, keep the tiller to starboard! We're not clear."

Courtney nodded, even as she started to unwind the mainsheet from the far winch.

"I'll deal with the mainsheet, you make sure we get out of this without getting hit—or hitting anyone." Valerie jumped into action. Out of the corner of her eye, she saw Sarah Doherty take the lead by several boat lengths, her blue and white spinnaker immaculately set. Valerie tore her eyes away, focusing instead on her cousins, who had taken the tiller back from their fool of a friend but still seemed to be blithely unaware of what they and their inept houseguest had just done—cost Valerie the race, the regatta, and the cup.

"Kathryn!" She shouted above the wind, as Courtney corrected course and they came alongside them. "William!"

Kat, who was currently skipper, and Will, with a hand on the jib sheet, turned to her.

"What the hell was that?"

"Sorry, Valerie!" Will yelled apologetically. "Sam's new to sailing."

"No shit, Sherlock!" Valerie eased the jib sheet. "Do you have a death wish?"

"Relax, Valerie," Kat called out in an annoyingly calm tone. "We didn't hit you, in the end. No harm, no foul."

"You didn't hit us because *we* got out of the way! Despite having right of way!" Valerie glared at her cousins. "You forced us to give up the lead!"

The houseguest opened his mouth to speak, but Valerie didn't care to hear some half-baked apology.

"You, shut up. And you," she pointed at Kat, "I want to see a 720. Now."

"What?" Kat held a hand up to her ear. They were no longer near enough to hear her clearly.

Valerie raised her voice even louder, howling like the very wind. "I said, shut up and spin!"

Will recoiled slightly, and even Kat seemed to flinch. The houseguest, however, had the expression of a man transfixed. Maybe she'd shocked him, with her intensity. Maybe he wasn't used to women who allowed themselves to be openly, vocally angry. Valerie didn't give a damn what he thought about her and her anger, and nor did she care if her cousins were scared, either. They'd just lost her not only the race, but the whole damn regatta. Everything she had worked her ass off to win.

Scowling, Valerie returned her attention to the sails. They were full, but there was no way she and Courtney were going to catch Sarah Doherty. Not unless they magically grew a motor. "*Fuck!*"

Courtney eyed her, sympathetically. "I know, I'm pissed, too." She paused. "Although, probably not as pissed as you."

Valerie whipped her head around. "What the hell is that supposed mean?"

"Nothing, cap. You just have your great uncle's rare but rarefied temper, that's all."

Uncle Willie. Valerie turned around, trying to catch a glimpse of her great uncle in the Woosters' boat. And there he was, watching the race with a pleasant smile on his face. He wouldn't know which boat she was, though. Not without her putting up her spinnaker. Then, Mac could tell him which color to look for.

Valerie sighed. "Alright, let's try that again."

"You want to put the spinnaker up? We've only got a few boat lengths left."

Valerie eyed the horizon. They were indeed almost at the finish.

The Best Crew

She could see the flag on the committee boat, hear Sarah's shrill cheer as race committee blew their horn to welcome the regatta's victor. "We're not giving up. I don't care how many boats have passed us, or if we can see the whites of the eyes of every person on that committee boat. Even if we lose, even if we're the last boat to the line, we fight like hell until we finish."

Courtney swallowed a sigh. "Aye, aye, captain."

Half an hour later, they stood on the yacht club's dock and surveyed the fleet, all the Ensigns in various stages of derigging. They'd finished fourth in the race, and third in the regatta. All because of those fucking fools she called cousins, and their idiotic and utterly inept houseguest.

"Well," Courtney said cheerily, perhaps sensing Valerie's stormy mood, "At least neither of us was injured."

Valerie remained silent, not trusting herself to speak.

"I mean, what with the series races starting tomorrow—"

"I know." Valerie glared at her cousins in the distance, securing the family Ensign to its mooring. They'd begged her to let them take it out for once, citing their houseguest's desire to race, and she'd agreed, because Courtney's parents were willing to sit the regatta out this year and let Courtney and Valerie sail their Ensign, *Moonbeam*, instead. "We were extremely lucky. I could have been on the bow and been knocked into the water, you could have been distracted and taken a hit to the head, not to mention the damage any collision might have done to *Moonbeam*—I just can't believe Kat and Will let that *idiot* take the tiller. It's outrageous. It's ridiculous. It's *dangerous*."

Courtney nodded, a touch warily. "Still, we're all okay. And the boat, too—"

"If you don't know how to sail, *don't!*" Abruptly, Valerie turned away from the thorofare, clutching the spinnaker bag to her chest. "I mean, honestly!" She closed her eyes, willing away weakness in the form of welling tears.

"Listen, I gotta get back. I promised my parents I would get lobsters for dinner and the soft shells with big claws are all gone by five." Courtney eyed Valerie. "Are you okay?"

"Fine," she bit out. "Just fine. No thanks to that fool."

Courtney nodded. "Do you want me to help you with the spinnaker bag?"

Valerie shook her head. "No." It wasn't that she didn't trust Courtney with the spinnaker, it was just that the extra sail was her specialty. And besides, re-organizing the bag might help her to cool down. "See you tomorrow."

"Noon?"

"Noon."

"Sam, could you pass me the sail ties?"

Sam jerked his head up, nearly knocking it against the boom in the process. "Sure, yeah, what do they look like?"

Kat pointed to a pile of purple and green strips of fabric, each a foot long and just about an inch wide. "That."

Nodding, Sam reached for the woven ties, gathering them together in one hand. "Do you think she'll be alright?"

"Who? Valerie?"

Sam shrugged, struggling to keep up with all the sailing talk. "The—what do you call it? The person steering?"

"The skipper," Kat provided. "She'll be fine."

"She looked..." Furious, fearsome, fiery... fetching?

"Pissed," Kat supplied. "She looked *pissed*. But that's fair, we did nearly put a hole in her hull, and besides, we cost her the cup."

Sam bit his lip. *Shit*. "I didn't mean to—"

"I know, Sam. And so does she. Well, not currently. But she will. We'll explain it to her, later, over a cocktail."

"Cocktails cure everything," Will announced, from his perch on the prow or the bow or, well, the front of the boat. He appeared to be folding the small sail that Sam had by now come to know as the jib. "Especially malaria."

Kat shook her head, apparently torn between amusement and exasperation. "No, Will, that's quinine."

"And is quinine not what makes a gin and tonic?" Will tied off a stray bit of rope.

The twins descended into a divisive discussion as to the correct ratio of gin to tonic, while Sam sat on the side of the boat and stared off into the distance.

If he were being honest with himself, he'd have to admit that he was watching for someone. Valerie, of the eyes filled with fury. And if he were to continue being honest with himself, he'd be forced to confess that the reason he was waiting and watching the wharf wasn't just because he didn't know how to derig an Ensign without explicit guidance from his now bickering hosts. His eyes were trained on the distant docks because of the myriad emotions Kat and Will's second cousin had inspired in him.

Sam felt incredibly guilty for causing the near collision that had apparently lost Valerie the race. And the regatta. He was embarrassed by his mistake, and he was ashamed of his inexperience. He should never have accepted the—what was it called?—the tiller. But Kat had handed it to him with such calm, such confidence. And Will had promised that steering was "the easy part of sailing."

But the tumult in Sam's stomach wasn't just a perfect storm of guilt, shame, and embarrassment. There was something else happening there. Everywhere, and all at once. Butterflies, not just fluttering but doing nosedives and backflips. Like some adventurous fleet of fighter planes in the middle of a war. Because there was a war, being waged within Sam's mind and body. A war between his feelings. There were those that were appropriate, like the shame and the guilt and the embarrassment. And then there were those that were utterly unacceptable, entirely inappropriate. Excitement, arousal, and a kind of musical thrill that tripped down the ladder of his spine. Valerie was on his mind.

Her dark braided hair, the severity of her nose, her lips like the petals of a windblown rose. And her eyes, beneath furrowed brows, flashing with fury and absent all fear as Sam, in the Abbotts' Ensign, had swerved too near.

"Could you reach belowdeck and find the sail cover?" Apparently Kat had finished her argument with Will. "It's that mass of blue canvas that, you know, covers the sail."

They finished derigging without further incident, and Sam tried to stow his feelings about Valerie safely away, to be examined and processed on another day. Kat announced, with a smirk, that because Sam had nearly dented another Ensign, he would be the one to row them back to the Abbott dock. Sam obliged without argument, although he suspected Kat had been joking and that either she or Will would have been happy to take up the oars themselves. Still, it felt right, to do some penance. And it's not like he didn't know how to row. Sam had rowed crew at Essex, briefly, and it had instilled in him a great love of being out on the water.

Will caught them as they met the dock, jumping onto the float with a length of rope. He then proceeded to perform some complex figure eight with the rope over and around the metal thing that Sam had heard called a cleat, as Sam and Kat clambered out of the rowboat. "I think it's time we had a drink," Will announced, admiring his handiwork.

Kat nodded fervently. "It's five o'clock somewhere."

Sam shook his head, but he couldn't keep a slight chuckle from escaping. "Why do I get the feeling I'll be in rehab by the end of my stay?"

Kat patted him on the shoulder, while Will led the way toward the ramp, which was as low as the tide was high. "It's an island, Sam. There's nothing to do, but sail and drink and sail and drink and sail and drink and—"

"And stargaze," added Will, dreamily, "and make s'mores and bike and explore—just not Widow's Woods—and swim and tan and go on the occasional boat picnic!"

Something wicked lit in Kat's eye. "That's right, there's always swimming."

Instinct told Sam to back away immediately. "Why do I get the feeling you don't mean—"

The last thing Sam saw was Kat's smirk, paired with Will's pitying smile, before he was falling—off the dock, and into the ice-cold water.

Sam came up shocked and spluttering, his ankle caught in what he hoped was seaweed. "Fuck!"

The twins erupted in laughter like they were fifteen again and raced up the ramp before Sam had the chance to pull himself up the swim ladder and wrestle either or both of them in. Well, it was what he deserved. To be sopping wet and freezing cold and alone. Still, he would find a way to fix this, to earn Valerie's forgiveness. She couldn't be made of stone.

Chapter 3
On Dry Land

Dressed in dry clothes, with a towel around his neck to catch any drips from his still-damp hair, Sam settled down on the couch. Kat was over by the stereo, thumbing through CDs in their plastic cases and records in dusty sleeves. Sam glanced around the low lit living room with a slight frown. "Where's Will?"

His host didn't bother to glance up from her perusing. "In the kitchen, no doubt arranging and rearranging the lime slices." She pulled a CD from the stack. "How do you feel about Ella Fitzgerald?"

Sam scoffed. "Do you think anyone would object to Ella?"

Kat nodded absently as she slipped the disc in to the stereo and hit the play button. Dreamy jazz began to filter through the speakers. "We grew up on her Cole Porter. Best rendition of his songbook, our grandfather always claimed."

"And he wasn't wrong." Will entered the living room carrying a tray of very tall, doubtless very strong gin and tonics. He set the square of lacquered wood down on the low table before the couch, plucking a highball from its resting place and handing it to Sam. The lime slice looked a little weary, indeed.

Sam accepted the glass, holding it up to clink against Will's own. "Cheers. And thank you, again, for having me."

Kat took up her glass and thrust it forward for Sam and Will to toast. "Nonsense," she replied dismissively. "The invitation was standing, and your visit was long overdue." She took a long draught of her drink, smiling. "Just strong enough," she announced approvingly.

Sam took a sip of his own, and immediately winced. "Strong is certainly the right word for it. Do you remember that time at school, when we accidentally bought grain alcohol off that townie?" He glanced at Will. "But Kat's pride wouldn't allow us to pour it down the drain, so we kept drinking?"

Will laughed. "I don't remember, actually. But I think that's because I drank the most of the three of us."

Kat shook her head sadly. "Never could hold his own, my baby brother."

Will opened his mouth but his protest was lost to the sound of Sam's laughter.

"We were what—fifteen?" Sam asked, when he had caught his breath.

Kat nodded.

Will shook his head, almost mournfully. "Can't believe we're twice the age we were then. It seems like yesterday."

"I thought you said you didn't remember it?" Kat raised an eyebrow.

Will raised both of his. "I don't remember that night. I *do* remember the morning after."

Sam watched the twins with fond amusement. "I have to say—" But then his phone rang, buzzing in his pocket. He pulled it out, checking the screen. "It's my mother; I'd better take it."

He stood, setting his gin and tonic back down on the tray, and stepped into the hallway. "Hello? Mom?"

"Honey! You're on speaker phone. Your father and I wanted to check and make sure you arrived okay. Was the drive long?"

"Not too bad, honestly. Kat was good company."

She hummed her approval. "We did something similar, when we were your age and just married—we drove up from Boston to go camping in Acadia! That's not far from you, actually. You're on Juniper, right?"

"Juniper Island, yes."

"Smack in the middle of midcoast Maine, if I recall correctly. How are the blueberries?"

Sam laughed. "I haven't had a chance to try one yet, but I imagine they're delicious."

"They're excellent with a little heavy cream," his father interjected, "for breakfast."

"Jonathan. You know you can't have heavy cream. Your cholesterol—"

"I'm not saying *I'm* going to have wild blueberries for breakfast with heavy cream. I'm saying our son should have blueberries for breakfast with a dash of heavy cream. Carol, you really must learn to listen."

Sam's mother scoffed. "Ignore your father," she said, simply. "Or don't! But one should always be wary of heart disease. And you're no spring chicken, Sam."

Sam's eyebrows shot up. "Me? I'm just thirty!"

"And that's when it starts. That's when your body begins to betray you… Limb by limb, organ by organ… But don't take my word for it, Sam. It's only that my doctor says—"

"We didn't call you to read you the riot act on high blood pressure, or whatever your mother's on about now," Sam's father cut in.

"I should hope not," Sam muttered beneath his mother's spluttered protest, although he was hardly surprised. She had always been a health nut.

"We just wanted to check in with you."

"We figured we'd call you, since it's been at least two weeks since you called us," his mother continued.

"Not that you're keeping track…"

"No! Of course not."

"Anyway, we'll let you go now." His father's tone was firm, and for that Sam was grateful. He loved his parents, but he didn't need to talk to them daily. And he had called his mother more recently than she claimed. Hadn't he?

His mother sighed. "Oh, alright. Goodnight, honey! Don't let the twins get you into trouble!" She still refused to believe that Sam was responsible for at least a third of their near-misses with the authorities during adolescence, be they academic or some form of law-enforcement.

Sam shook his head, smothering a laugh. "Goodnight, Mom! Night, Dad. Love you lots." They said their farewells and he hung up the phone, slipping it back into his pocket. Then, Sam strolled back into the living room, where Kat and Will were arguing about something that was no doubt insignificant.

Sam settled back into his seat on the couch, between his friends. They continued to argue, across him. Sam frowned, wondering how he could put an end to their bickering. Not permanently, as it did amuse him, but for now. Inspiration struck in the form of a sailboat painting, hanging on the wall above the old fashioned television. "Hey, can one of you explain this whole racing situation to me?"

Kat and Will snapped to attention.

Will cocked his head. "What do you mean?"

"Like, how to sail? Or, what happened today? Because neither of us is skilled enough to teach you how to sail, and what happened today feels fairly self-explanatory."

Sam laughed, running his hand through his drying hair. "No, I mean, can you, like, contextualize today's race for me? Was it a one-off?"

Kat pursed her lips. "Well, it clearly wasn't a one-off, given that we sailed the same course several times and the winner was chosen based on a cumulative score. It was a regatta."

Sam narrowed his eyes slightly. "So... are there a lot of regattas?"

"No," Will jumped in, lowering his glass. "Regattas are special occasions."

"Most of the racing on island is done in a series," Kat continued when it became clear her brother would not be elaborating, "which is, as the name suggests, a series of individual races for a specific class of boats. Each race counts and your cumulative score determines your place in the series—whether you win or not, basically. It's the opposite of a one-shot, kind of like a regatta over the course of a month."

"And these are popular?"

Kat nodded. "There isn't one in June, since not enough sailors are on island, but there's the July Series, which is fairly competitive, and the August Series, which starts tomorrow and is the most popular—because so many summer folk are on island—and also the most competitive, since among those summer folk are some of the best sailors on the East Coast."

Sam raised his eyebrows.

"No joke. Some of these people have been sailing all their lives. Sixty years on the water, in the same class of boats, with an array of competitors, older and younger. It keeps them on their toes. Valerie's that kind of sailor, the kind who cares a lot about winning and spends all her free time practicing—when she's not teaching. That's why she was so upset when you ruined her race."

Sam winced. "I feel so bad…"

"Yeah, it's weird because I thought she'd come for cocktails and we could all grovel the whole time at her feet, while the alcohol softened her heart," Kat shrugged, "but apparently she's still too pissed to come over. I texted her, but no answer."

Sam bit his lip. "I should go find her, and tell her that I'm sorry. Again."

Will shook his head, his eyes wide.

Kat laughed. "That, my friend, is the gin talking."

Sam looked down and found he'd finished most of his drink, which had to have been a double.

"Valerie does not like visitors, during the day or at night. She's private, alright?"

"Fair," he said, nodding. "But I'll find a way to make it right."

The Best Crew

"Valerie might not like to receive visitors," Will offered, his eyes on the dark lawn beyond the living room window, "but she does like to visit."

"What?" Kat followed his gaze. "Oh..."

Sam stood and went to the window. "What are you two looking at?"

And then he saw it. Her, rather. Not a ghost, but a girl. A woman, crossing the lawn with an old flashlight in hand. He squinted, trying to make out Valerie's features in the low light of the sunset. "Where is she going?"

"To visit our grandfather. Her great uncle, but he's like a grandfather to her. They're really close, even with his dementia. Always have been."

"She likes to talk to him," Will added. "Tells him about her day, especially if there's been a race."

Kat sighed. "We should really do the same. But not tonight. I wouldn't want to disturb Valerie and Granddad's time together. It means a lot to her." Kat stood, abruptly, and picked up the tray. "Another cocktail, anyone?"

The sun had crossed the horizon as Valerie shut the cabin door. She hadn't been able to see it, since she'd been facing the woods, but she'd noticed the shift in the light on the trees, in the angle of the orange light, as the sun disappeared for the night. Still, the lingering rays lit the woods as she walked through them, and illuminated the great lawn as she crossed its expanse.

Through the window of the East Wing's living room, she could see the vague shapes of her cousins on the worn couch, and someone —their inept houseguest, no doubt—standing in the window. Her invitation to cocktails was unspoken and longstanding, although a text from Kat suggested that Valerie's cousins were not lacking in self-awareness, regarding their earlier idiocy, and wanted to make amends over a bottle of Hendrick's.

Valerie was in no mood to be plied with liquor—and lots of it, considering the length of her cousin's pour—paired with profuse apologies, whose sincerity would nevertheless fail to satisfy her anger. What kind of fools gave the tiller to a novice? Ensigns were large, unwieldy boats and that kind of carelessness could do a lot of damage to property and persons.

Shaking her head, Valerie sighed and averted her eyes from the East Wing's window. She needed a night to cool off. In the morning, when all was calm and well, she would have the necessary conversation with her cousins—and their guest—about water safety and the risks inherent to the sport.

For now, she just wanted to relax, to step out of her metaphorical sailing boots and get her land legs back. Visiting her Uncle Willie would help with that, which is why she was currently crossing the lawn to the old West Wing with its new extension.

Valerie had texted Tessa, her great uncle's nurse and companion, to let her know she was coming. She could have showed up unannounced, and she often did, but it was getting late and she didn't want to disturb her great uncle if he was in the process of winding down for the night.

Feeling some of the weight lift from her shoulders at the sight of the West Wing, with its worn steps and recently reinforced railing leading up to its dark green painted door, Valerie felt a small smile curve the corners of her lips. She knocked, once, hoping she could be heard over the television whose faint but familiar chaos was audible from the steps.

From within, her great uncle asked, "What's that?"

Someone—Tessa, presumably—stood and crossed over to the door. Valerie could hear her footsteps on the hardwood floor. "Your great niece, captain. Valerie." Tessa opened the door, smiling at Valerie. "Come on in. We're just watching an episode of *Hogan's Heroes*."

Huffing a laugh at the predictability of her great uncle's preferences, Valerie stepped into the well-lit West Wing. It had been renovated, slightly, and the furniture had been rearranged and in some cases replaced to better accommodate her great uncle's reduced mobility and increasingly regular bouts of confusion, but it was still familiar to her, an anchor of sorts—binding her fast, in memory, to the summer evenings of her childhood, when she and her cousins had come over to the West Wing for desert and a rambunctious round of cards.

It hadn't mattered to her great uncle that she wasn't his granddaughter. It hadn't mattered to Valerie that her own, more immediate family was... well, messy. To the extent that she took refuge with slightly more distant relations. It had only mattered that they—Valerie, Kat, Will, Uncle Willie, and whoever else was around that night—were all of them family, and that they had fresh blueberry grunt and one pack of playing cards per person.

Still more vivid, in her mind, were the mornings she had spent in the small kitchen here as a teenager, scheming with her great uncle about tides and starts and tactics, before they two went out to race in the August Series.

Valerie had spent the whole year, as a kid, looking forward to those series races. They allowed her to spend time with her favorite person in the world and, not only that, but to make him proud of her. Her Uncle Willie had taught Valerie everything she knew about sailing, had inspired her to teach it, too—because of how fun he'd made it, how seriously he took her, how much she'd loved their shared time out on the water.

Thanks to his dementia, Uncle Willie's racing days were behind him. Valerie had been tasked with taking the tiller in hand, shouldering her great uncle's legacy as skipper of his vessel while making a name for herself as a sailor, too. She'd found a new sailing partner, a willing crew. And together they'd met with success, winning several of the past years' series as well as many of the standalone races. It wasn't the same, but it was something. Something worth fighting for—

a rock, when all the rest of her world, of her life, seemed built on sand.

"Valerie!"

"Uncle Willie! How's Hogan? Has he managed to escape the POW camp yet?"

Her great uncle shook his white-haired head. "No, not yet. But he will. He will..."

She nodded, lowering herself into the armchair beside his. "He always does."

"Did you race today?"

Anticipating a conversation, Tessa reached for the remote.

Valerie bit her lip, her eyes on the now frozen screen. "Yes, and you were out there, watching. Mac took you out in the Woosters' boat."

Uncle Willie nodded, but she wondered if he actually remembered. "Bring home any trophies?"

"You know full well they don't award us any trophies until the Summer's End Tea."

Her great uncle chuckled. "That wasn't a no."

Valerie smiled at Uncle Willie, who smiled back. She allowed herself to revel in the warmth of his affection. Its refusal to fade felt like a small miracle in the face of his dementia. "Sarah Doherty won, actually. I tried, but..." She didn't want to burden him with the knowledge of her cousins' irreverent interference. "You can't win every race!"

Uncle Willie eyed her thoughtfully, his expression an echo of the precision, the perception, the profound understanding he'd possessed in his earlier years. "*You* can."

Valerie laughed, but not because his words didn't mean the world to her. "Clearly not. Besides, all my victories are yours."

Confusion clouded his narrowed eyes.

"I only win," she clarified, "because of you. Your instruction. So, when I win, it's like old times. You're right there with me."

Except that wasn't really true. Increasingly, Valerie felt... alone.

Lonely. Sailing was her respite, her refuge, but... victories should be shared with someone, or else they were empty. Cold. Valerie was fond of her current crew, a capable sailor who knew when to shut up and what to do, but... It wasn't the same as sailing with someone she loved. Someone who loved her.

Valerie inhaled sharply and blinked back the few tears that had threatened to spill over. Brightening, she turned to her great uncle. "Shall we watch the rest of the episode?"

Chapter 4
Hardcore Harding

The next morning, a somewhat hungover Sam decided it would be in his best interest to go for a light jog. Waving away Kat's bleary-eyed offer of coffee, because that was the last thing his empty stomach needed, as well as Will's highly recommended but hardly tempting hair-of-the-dog, Sam laced up his sneakers and found an old baseball cap, then set off to get lost.

Town, it turned out, was so small that getting lost was impossible. And Sam didn't trust his legs, which were still stuck in sea-mode, to make it up the many hills that led out of town in the direction of the public tennis courts, the island school, the grocery store, and the small harbor all the way on the other side of Juniper. So, he stayed in the town circuit, running laps around the one-way loop, passing the ferry terminal and the public landing and the path leading down to the private docks where the yacht club was located and out of which the surprisingly robust—as described by Kat—summer sailing program operated.

Sam was tempted to stop at the gift shop, but it was closed until ten, and he hadn't brought his wallet anyway. Instead, he found himself doubling back to the entrance to the yacht club—a flight of stony stairs with one rickety railing, leading down to the private docks and their attached floats. He didn't know why he was so drawn to this place, which should have been barred to him after that disaster of a race, but the stairs were inviting, worn as they were, and he caught a glimpse of some unexpected color on the wall at the bottom of the slope.

Glancing around, Sam saw no one. It was a figurative, if not literal, according to Will, ghost town. Therefore, he decided to investigate. Sam took the stairs two at a time and afterward figured he'd been lucky not to fall.

Posted on a slab of wood that doubled as the wall of a waterfront house and, apparently, a message board, were countless pieces of tacked up paper. Some were so old that they had faded in the weeks, or possibly years, since their posting, but others were newer, brighter, drawn in marker or printed in dark ink. There were handwritten advertisements for private sailing lessons, private tennis lessons, private rowing lessons. There were printed schedules for tournaments and clinics: tennis, doubles tennis, golf—Sam hadn't realized the island was big enough for a course. Someone was currently selling a dinghy, and another person wanted to buy or rent an Ensign for the summer before last. As Sam traced the letters on the signs, he suddenly heard someone sigh.

"Not you again."

Sam spun around, his heart racing—no doubt because of the surprise. When he'd recovered his composure, he replied, "Valerie, right?"

She nodded and Sam saw that, where there had once been nothing but fury in her eyes, this morning she looked... tired. And a little sad, too.

"Are you—"

Valerie leveled him with a look. "Am I what? Going to yell at you a little more?" The anger was returning, bringing color to her cheeks.

Sam shook his head, swallowing. "I just meant to ask—You don't look—Are you alright?"

She pushed past him, a piece of paper in hand. "I'm fine," she said, stiffly. "Not that it's any of your business. Is that my great uncle's hat?"

"Maybe." Over her shoulder, he could just make out the block letters across the top of the red piece of paper she held against the wall.

WANTED: CREW FOR AUGUST SERIES.

Valerie pulled a couple of tacks out of her pocket and stuck—stabbed, rather—them through the corners of the paper and into the multipurpose wall. "There," she muttered. "That'll get their attention."

Sam cocked his head. "Whose attention?"

"Are you still standing there?" She shot him a withering glance over her shoulder. "Lurking?"

"Yes," Sam said sincerely before he could think better of it. "I ended my run early just so I could lie in wait here for you."

Valerie scoffed. On her, his little joke was lost. Well, Sam doubted she'd missed it. Perhaps she just wasn't feeling particularly playful, after yesterday's fiasco.

Sam returned his attention to the sign she'd just posted. "Why do you need crew?"

She sighed again, and that weariness returned to her eyes. "I shouldn't have to explain myself to you." And with that, she stalked off in the direction of the club house.

Sam started to follow her. She didn't bother to turn, just shook her head. Over the sound of a lobster boat's engine revving to life, she called, "Casino members only!" And then, more quietly, but still loudly enough for the sound to carry across the still waters and stiller dock, "AKA, fuck off."

Sam shrugged, still feeling quite guilty about having cost her the race, but determined to be in a good mood. It was, after all, a bright and clear morning. Not a cloud in the sky, and the bees already busy in the flower-boxes of the houses that looked out over the docks. He made his way back up the stone steps, through town, and all the way up the Abbott driveway. As he opened the door to the East Wing kitchen, he was met by his hosts, who had made a fresh pot of coffee. Will had an air of concern about him, while Kat's lips were pressed into a permanent frown.

"What's up?"

"How was your run?" Kat offered him a cup.

Accepting the coffee, Sam wiped some drying sweat from his temple with the hem of his shirt. "More of a jog. I ran into Valerie, actually. She said something about a casino?"

"That's just what the yacht club is called. It's a historical term, there's no gambling." *That they know of*, he half expected Kat to add.

"And so did we. Run into Valerie, I mean." Will frowned, his hunched shoulders and rounded eyes radiating worry. "She stopped by on her way into town."

Kat started to refill her own cup. "Apparently, there's been an accident. In addition to the demise of Valerie's coffee maker."

"An accident?" Valerie had looked well, if tired, when he'd seen her. Except... there had been something in her expression, a weariness that didn't seem to equate to mere tiredness. "What do you mean?"

Will sighed. "Valerie's sailing partner was in a biking accident this morning, early. One of the dawn circuits. She shattered her wrist."

"Well, they don't *know* that. The clinic doesn't have the resources to do an x-ray." Kat sipped her coffee, looking uncharacteristically grave. "But she'll be on the first boat back to the mainland this morning, and then off to Camden, where they'll get a good look. She'll be fine, I'm sure, but it's a bitch."

"For more reasons than one..." Will added, mournfully.

Kat nodded. "I mean, don't get me wrong, I'm really sorry about what's happened to Courtney. Court's a friend, and an injury like this... It hurts like hell, it's inconvenient, it's expensive... But she didn't hit her head, and she's going to be alright. Plus, she's got good insurance."

Sam frowned. "I don't understand. How is that more than one reason?"

Kat and Will exchanged a meaningful glance. "Well... Court's injury means Valerie's out of a partner in the Juniper Island August Series. And no one on this island wants to crew for her."

Will sipped his coffee in sorrowing silence.

Sam didn't understand. "Why? Isn't she, like, the best sailor here?"

Smirking, Kat said, "Yeah, but she's also a bit of a bitch in the boat." She shrugged. "I mean, I love her to death. Favorite cousin, no question. But the other sailors on this island? The ones who aren't already committed to skipper or crew? They don't want to race the August Series with Valerie."

"Why not?"

"Do I really have to spell it out for you?" Kat snorted. "They're scared of her."

"Why?" Sam wasn't scared of Valerie. Sure, she seemed... stormy. And strong, and smart, and, admittedly, a bit sexy when she was angry. But she had to be a decent person, or else Kat and Will wouldn't love her so much. And maybe being a good sailor meant putting safety—not to mention, victory—ahead of demureness or docility. Maybe the best sailors were a bit scary. And maybe that was why they won.

"I just feel bad for Valerie," Will said, sighing.

"Surely she'll find someone to crew for her...?"

Will shook his head while Kat explained. "Not by noon, when the skippers have to turn in the names of their crew to race committee. And even if they extended the deadline, she still couldn't get it done by the first gun, which is at one. She's screwed. And this series, it means a lot to her..."

"She just needs someone," Will murmured. "Anyone..."

An idea popped into Sam's head, just then. Possibly ill-advised. But ill-advised ideas were his specialty. "What about me?"

Kat's brows knit. "What about you?"

"I can crew." That was verb, right? He was saying that correctly, wasn't he? Because Kat and Will were both looking at him like he'd spouted pure nonsense. Then, when the silence stretched and it became apparent that he wasn't joking, Kat threw her head back and started to laugh.

"You? Crew for Valerie?"

Sam shrugged. "Maybe I can make it up to her, in the process. Yesterday, I mean. Maybe if I help her win this series or whatever, she'll forgive me." For some reason, Sam really really wanted Valerie to forgive him. Besides, he liked being useful.

Will and Kat exchanged another meaningful glance. Kat turned back to Sam and narrowed her eyes. "It's certainly an idea..."

"James, please. You know I never beg, but... I am begging you."

Her friend and coworker shook his head. "I apologize, Valerie. But Estie wants to learn to sail."

"And you can't teach her on Sundays?"

James frowned. "Sundays are for boat picnics, you know that. Besides, Estie wants to race."

Valerie bit her lower lip. "Fuck, man. What am I going to do?"

"Have you asked—"

"I've asked *everyone*. I've even promised payment in the form of second-hand romance novels and my firstborn son." The Casino didn't let you pay your crew in anything so vulgar as money. Not that Valerie had as unlimited a supply as her cousins, besides.

"You haven't asked *everyone*," an all-too-familiar voice whispered in Valerie's ear.

Valerie didn't flinch, but she did mutter a curse. "Think of the devil and she shall appear!"

Kat feigned affront. "I'm here as your guardian angel, coz. But I'm flattered and unsurprised to find out that I was on your mind. I am helpful, aren't I?"

Valerie turned to face her cousin, her hands automatically finding her hips. "Oh? Because this morning I seem to recall both you and Will refusing to come to my aid."

"Well, you're not Gondor and the fate of Middle-earth is not at stake."

Valerie glared at Kat. "You're such a nerd. How is comparing my situation to a fictional fantasy movie trilogy helping?"

This time, Kat appeared to take actual offense. "That was a book reference! But if you don't want my help..."

Valerie sighed and forcibly put her skepticism aside. This was her cousin. Her favorite cousin. If she couldn't trust *her*... "What kind of help?"

Kat's eyes were bright. "I've found someone for you."

Valerie immediately perked up, causing Kat to smirk.

"See? Not so unhelpful or devilish after all."

Valerie flexed her fingers impatiently. "Who? Who have you found?"

"Whom," James interjected, automatically.

Valerie sent him a withering glance. "Say hi to your girlfriend for me, traitor. And I know it's 'whom.' I do still happen to be an English teacher."

"Traitor? Because I am choosing to spend time with the one I love over..." James looked her over. "A biting wit and bitterness?" He shook his head, apologized again, and strode away.

Valerie huffed, turning back to her cousin. "Who is it, Kat? I've asked *everyone*. Not even my students want to sail with me."

"Probably because you're terrifying, and mean. And they have better ways to spend their Saturdays."

Valerie scoffed. "I'm not mean. I just... I just know how to sail, okay?"

"Mmm," Kat gave her a skeptical once-over. "Well, I suppose that's true. Enough for both you and your crew, I'd argue."

"Well, yeah. I guess I could take someone on who isn't really that familiar with—"

"Excellent. I'll tell him you're in." Kat made to leave, but Valerie grabbed her sleeve.

"Wait a second..." Valerie's mind was starting to whir, as if in the presence of danger.

"Come on, it'll be good!" Kat flashed a wicked smile, twisting free of her cousin's grip. "You'll have *fun*."

And then it clicked. Valerie's arm fell to her side as her whole body went numb. "No. No, no, no, *no*. Not after yesterday."

Kat gave a rare pout. "Please, Valerie? Yesterday was an accident. Besides, he's had a really rough go of it lately and learning to sail would lift his spirits."

"Yeah, because—how long did you say he was staying with you? A month?—yeah, a month's vacation in Maine is hard."

"Valerie."

"What? He looked fine this morning." He had looked more than fine, wearing tight running shorts and a faint sheen of sweat like it was a fashionable accessory, but she wasn't about to dwell on any traitor instincts. The Victorians had been right. Repress, repress, repress. "It's me you should be worried about."

Kat waved away this last statement with a flick of her wrist. "Well, he's not fine. Not entirely."

"I don't need any drama on my boat," Valerie warned. This was a terrible idea, and she refused to sign on to it. Especially if there was even more wrong with this man than he'd demonstrated during yesterday's race.

"And you won't get any! Sam doesn't let the cracks show."

"Kat, look. You're family. But that doesn't mean I'll do just anything for you."

Kat made a face. "Doesn't it, though? Oh, come on. Who's always been here for you? Since day one?"

Valerie crossed her arms over her chest. "The only reason you were at the hospital that night was because your brother had a fever and your mother couldn't find a babysitter."

"That, and so that I could witness the birth of my soon-to-be favorite cousin!"

"Stretching it. You were three." But even as she spoke, reality hit like a boom to the head. Her day had been one long, continuous death roll, and she wasn't sure how many more metaphorical capsizes she could survive. Looking out at the fleet, at the boats with their sails half-hoisted, Valerie sighed. It was nearly noon. "We're wasting time. And I don't really have a choice, do I?"

Kat shook her head. "Not unless you want to forfeit the series."

"The world would have to be ending for me back out of a race."

Her cousin huffed a laugh. "That's exactly what I told Sam."

"And you or Will can't—"

Kat shook her head firmly. "I'm not a sailor, beyond our great-grandfather's regatta. And as for Will... Well, he's my brother, and I love him, but..."

"He did once jump off a boat in the middle of the race to swim with the seals." Valerie swore loudly, startling a seagull. "Fine. I'll take your inept houseguest. But only because there's literally no other option."

"Forfeit's technically still on the table..."

"As I said, *literally* no other option." Valerie glared at her cousin. "And for the record, I'd like to point out that I teach for a living. The series is supposed to be my refuge, my escape, my break. But, no, because Courtney broke her wrist, and because apparently this island is populated by cowards—"

"People can hear you, Valerie..." Kat glanced around the dock, in amusement rather than alarm.

"What are they going to do? Refuse to crew for me? Oh, wait, they already have. En masse." She sighed. "Run up to the compound and tell this Sam of yours to meet me down here in ten. And remind him that this isn't some boozy, bougie pleasure cruise. It's a race. He should conduct himself accordingly." Valerie tightened her ponytail. "I'll submit our names to race committee."

Kat smiled triumphantly. "His last name is Parsons. Samuel Parsons. And you won't regret this."

Valerie cast one last baleful look at her cousin, then dragged her feet in the direction of the club house, muttering, "Oh, but I will."

"Who?"

Pinching the bridge of her nose, Valerie repeated herself. "Samuel Parsons."

Mr. Hays, the commodore of the Juniper Island Casino, narrowed his eyes curiously. "And where did you find him?"

"He's a guest of the Abbott twins," she replied, hoping that would be the end of the questions.

"Ah." Recognition lit the old man's eyes. "Your cousins."

"Yep!" Valerie forced a smile. "So if that's everything…"

"Wait a minute." Mr. Hays frowned. "Isn't he the one who caused that collision?"

Valerie ground her teeth together at the reminder. "There was no collision."

Mr. Hays nodded. "That's right. My son says you jibed out of the way. And in doing so, lost the race!"

She exhaled slowly. Carefully. And then she forced another tight smile. "I can't win them all, I've been told." That was bullshit, though.

The commodore laughed. "No, but you want to. I can see the fire in your eyes, still. You remind me of your great uncle. You know, there was a summer back in—must've been '08, not so long ago—when your great uncle won every single Herreshoff race this island had to offer. He won the July Series, the Independence Day Regatta, the Candle Rock Race, the August Series, the Wooster Round, even the old Hurricane's Eye. And there was an actual hurricane that year, too! Nearly sank the fleet. But your great uncle never turned back."

Valerie swallowed, hard. It was difficult to talk about the good old days, before Uncle Willie's diagnosis and subsequent decline. "I know, Mr. Hays. I was in the boat with him."

"Ah, that's right! And at the Summer's End Tea, afterwards!" The old man beamed. "I thought I remembered you, and your cousins, scurrying up to collect all the prizes. Why, that August Series trophy was almost as big as you were, at the time!"

Valerie nodded. She remembered it all too well. "Right, well, if you'll excuse me—"

Mr. Hays placed the pen and the sign up sheet on the table. "Of course, you've got some rigging to do!" He checked his watch. "And quickly, too, if you want to get in any practice runs. You know, your great uncle always did like to test-run his spinnaker."

Forcing a third and final smile, Valerie turned and hurried toward the door. She wasn't sailing with Uncle Willie anymore. She was on her own—no, worse, she was saddled with a crew who probably had never even heard of a spinnaker, much less knew how to set one. And it wasn't like she could trust him to safely take the tiller, while she dealt with the extra sail. Christ, but Valerie was screwed. Except she refused to lose.

"I'll see you out on the water, Miss Harding!"

"See you later, sir." Squinting, she stepped out of the dimly lit club house and into the sunshine that seemed to mock her mood. The deed was done. She and the inept houseguest were stuck together for the entire series. Valerie had a sudden urge to turn, take the offending document up off the table, and tear it in two. Even as she worked to master herself, however, the true object of her ire appeared.

He was smiling, in a friendly sort of way, free of care as he strolled down the dock to meet her. His eyes were blue as the surrounding sea and his wheat blond hair was hidden away beneath that hat—Uncle Willie's hat.

"They let me down here after all," he announced amiably, by way of a greeting. "Or at least, nobody stopped me—"

"You shouldn't be wearing that," she snapped.

His brows knit. "What?"

"That hat. It's not yours." By rights, it should have been hers.

He smoothed the sun-bleached brim, the baby blue nearly white after years of wear and tear and exposure. "Ah, right. But I didn't bring one, and Kat said I ought to have something on my head. Keep the sun off my face, and all."

Bells from the island's lone church rang in the distance, marking the midday with their tired toll. Too late to turn back and tear up the sign up sheet. And considering the fact that she refused to forfeit... Valerie supposed she should pick her battles, or else the war would wear her down. "Whatever. Just don't lose it."

Sam smiled again, and Valerie was sure someone else would have found it charming. Someone with a weak mind and a will that was weaker still. "I don't intend to. Now, Val. How about—"

"No." She turned on her heel and started to walk in the direction of the dinghy float, both sides of which were cluttered with small boats.

Behind her, she heard him jog to catch up. "What? You didn't even let me finish my qu—"

Valerie spun around, and for the second time in two days Samuel Parsons nearly collided with her. This time, however, she didn't have the luxury of distance. This time, she could feel his body's heat, smell his deodorant—spiced and a little bit sweet. Shoving this new knowledge to the side, she held up one finger in warning. "Do not call me 'Val.'"

He shrugged. "Alright, Harding. How about we—"

She cocked her head, hoping the alternative angle would help her to understand him better. "Do you have an aversion to my name?"

Sam shook his head, affecting innocence. "No, I just have a fondness for nicknames." He grinned stupidly and Valerie wanted to groan. "In fact, I've already got yours. Wanna hear it?"

"Absolutely not."

His stupid grin turned shit-eating. "Hardcore Harding."

Valerie rolled her eyes. "Fine then. We'll forgo first names. If you promise not to add any adjectives or appellations." Without waiting for his answer, she led the way down the ramp, then down the float, all the way to the little rowboat dubbed *Humpty* that bobbed in some long-forgotten wake. "Get in the boat, Parsons."

He frowned. "Shouldn't I, I dunno, untie us first?"

Valerie shot him a withering look. "Can you identify the painter for me?"

Sam cocked his head curiously. He wasn't smiling, but there was a glimmer of humor in his bright blue eyes. It was irrepressible, rendering him incorrigible. "Painter? Like Frank Benson? I didn't realize he'd painted boats, as well, but I suppose it's not entirely out of left field. I mean, he did tend toward seaside scenes."

"*No.*" Although, Benson was her favorite artist. Valerie decided not to dwell on coincidence.

"No, he didn't paint lots of pretty little coastal pictures? Harding, are you unfamiliar—"

"With Benson? Hardly. Now, back to boats. The painter, also known as the bow line, is the length of rope that secures the vessel to the dock. It stems from the bow." She pointed. "This painter is currently tied to that metal ring using a bowline."

Sam frowned. "Okay, that terminology is confusing. Or maybe it's just the pronunciation?"

Ignoring him, she added, "I'll teach you about knots after the race, assuming I haven't marooned you on a rock in the thorofare before returning to the mooring."

Sam narrowed his eyes playfully. "I thought there weren't any rocks in the thorofare."

Valerie forced a wide smile, hoping it looked as unnerving as it felt. "There aren't. I hope you can swim!"

Without waiting for his response, she half-helped, half-shoved him into the boat. He sat down hard on the lone bench and, after recovering his balance, began to position the oars in the rust-ridden oarlocks. Valerie untied the painter, coiled it very casually, and tossed it into the bottom of the boat. Then she stepped into the little dinghy herself, balancing her weight against his automatically.

"Row," she commanded, once she was comfortably perched on the bow.

The oars sluiced the salt water. His form wasn't awful, she supposed, as he maneuvered them out of the crowded float area and in the direction of the fleet. And it was refreshing, to be rowed rather than to row. Valerie guessed she could get used to this.

Sam paused, his long fingers curled around the wooden shafts, beneath the polished grips. "Where to?"

She pointed over his shoulder to the red sailboat that was moored halfway between the yacht club and the Abbott dock. It was a familiar sight, a friendly face. Her first love and her best friend in many a race. "Try not to hit anything."

Chapter 5
Girlfriend

The oars were a little short, and the shafts looked and felt vaguely splintery, but Sam did his best to keep the boat moving in the right direction, with the bare minimum of input from Valerie. She was silent for the better part of the journey, silent and still, like one of those pretty wooden mermaids they had on pirate ships—except she was facing the wrong way and she wasn't topless. And, as per usual, she looked pissed.

"Don't go through that mooring."

Sam frowned. "What?"

Valerie pointed behind him, and he turned to look. There were two buoys, about five feet apart. One had a stick coming out the top, similar to the lobster pots he'd seen from the ferry, and the other was rounded like a red beach ball. "They're connected. If we were in a sailboat, especially one with a keel—that's the dagger-like extension on the bottom of the boat that keeps it from constantly capsizing—we'd get caught on the line between them."

"But right now we're in a rowboat. Flat-bottomed, I presume."

Valerie sighed, not bothering to hide her exasperation. "It's good practice, Parsons."

"Okay." Sam dug the right oar in a little deeper, maneuvering the boat around the beach ball. When they were clear of the mooring, he corrected his course. "The red one, right?"

Valerie nodded. "*Girlfriend.*"

Sam whipped his head back around. "I'm sorry, *what?*"

Her lips flickered in a suppressed smile, and Sam couldn't help but stare. It was the first time he'd seen her... well, happy was too strong a word, but maybe amused? Her brown eyes were bright for a second, before she shuttered them, brimming with... was that mischief?

"My great uncle loved sailing, more than anything—other than his family, of course. He'd spend whole summers out on the water but, when asked, he'd always say he'd been out with his girlfriend. All day, every day."

A startled laugh escaped Sam's throat. "What did his wife have to say about this?"

Valerie's lips curved again, her smile sweeter and no longer subtle. "Great Aunt Melissa knew better than to stand in the way of true love." Her smile widened as she huffed a little laugh. "They were married for fifty—Sam! Don't hit that boat!"

Sam had stopped steering, so stunned was he by the sight of Valerie's fond smile, the sound of her loving laughter. With a jolt, he jabbed the left oar down and out, slowing the little rowboat down and steering it narrowly to the side of a navy blue sailboat occupied by two elderly women who were watching him with amusement as they hoisted their sails.

"Found yourself a crew, then, Valerie?" The woman nearest to them raised her grey brows.

Valerie grimaced politely, but Sam wondered how anyone could mistake that for a smile, especially now that he'd seen the real thing. "Yes, Mrs. Wooster."

"Good-looking," the other woman mused, her eyes narrowing in the shade of her pink visor, and Sam felt his cheeks grow warm. "But does he know port from starboard?"

"Of course, Mrs. Adams," Valerie ground out, even as Sam

opened his mouth to confess that, in fact, he did not. She sent him a look that clearly communicated her desire for him to remain silent. Assessing the situation to the best of his abilities, Sam decided to do as he was told.

The two women laughed, but not unkindly. Shaking her head, Mrs. Wooster resumed her hoisting. "My dear, you must introduce us —but wait until after the race. Betty and I are off to do a practice run with our new spinnaker."

Valerie nodded, and signaled for Sam to row on. "We'll see you at the start, then, Mrs. Wooster. Mrs. Adams."

"Not if we see you first!"

Mrs. Wooster cackled at Mrs. Adams' joke. At least, Sam assumed it was a joke? He didn't know much about sailing, or starts. Still, he smiled at the two women as he rowed past their boat, and was rewarded for it when Mrs. Adams returned a smirk and a slightly wicked wink.

"Oh, for fuck's sake."

Bewildered, Sam turned to face Valerie, whose grimace was gone, replaced by a more honest—and increasingly familiar—glare. "What?"

"Just because an old woman flirts with you doesn't mean you have to flirt back. Honestly!"

He laughed and allowed himself to lean a little closer to her. "Would you rather I save my smiles for you, and only you?"

Valerie rolled her eyes. "I would rather you grab hold of the boat."

Sam straightened. "What boat?"

"Uncle Willie's *Girlfriend*. She's directly behind you. *Before* you hit her, thank you."

Sam quickly dropped the oars and turned in his seat, catching the raised wooden trim along the side of the crimson-hulled sailboat.

"Go on, climb in. I'll secure *Humpty*." She waited for him to stand and hoist himself up onto the Herreshoff. "Wait. Are you wearing *flip-flops*?"

Sam froze, midway between boats. "Yes?"

"No. Next time, if there is a next time, because I'm still not entirely convinced that you won't manage to kill us somehow, you need to wear closed-toe boat shoes. It's a matter of safety."

Sam shrugged. "Sure thing, Harding." Then he slid awkwardly into the cockpit, or whatever the cavity was called. "Do you need a hand—" But as he turned, he discovered that she was already in the boat. Standing so close, he could feel the warmth of her body, distinct from the warmth of the sun; smell the shampoo she used, rosemary and a hint of mint mingling with the salt air and the scent of wood varnish.

Their eyes met for a long second. Sam was lost in her irises' dark depths, like the shadows that played out against the bark of the pine trees that formed forests around the Abbott property. What secrets did they keep?

Valerie swayed a little with the sea, and Sam instinctively reached out to catch her by the waist. As soon as his fingers brushed against her side, she closed her eyes—and Sam would have sworn before the highest court that she leaned, ever so slightly, into his touch.

But before he could do anything about it, before he could do more than merely observe the soft curve of her waist beneath her worn t-shirt, they both went stumbling sideways, catching themselves on the stationary boom.

"What the hell was that?" Startled, and a little disgruntled to have been awoken from what now felt like a daydream, blown away by the ocean breeze, Sam glanced around in confusion and concern. "Are you alright?"

Valerie righted herself, then shook her head. "It was just a bit of wake." She nodded in the direction of a motorboat, blazing through the thorofare at a surely illegal speed. "Don't lean on the boom."

Sam removed his hands from the sail cover and opened his mouth to ask, "What now?" But Valerie was already moving.

"Don't just stand there," she said, her tone as brisk as the water that surrounded them. She pulled a stop watch out of her pocket and hung it round her neck. "We have twenty minutes before the starting gun. That's twenty minutes for me to rig this boat, teach you the basics, and hopefully get in at least one practice run. Don't ask me about starts, because we don't have time to go over them. You'll just have to trust me. And do exactly what I say." She met his eyes at last, almost reluctantly. "Okay?"

Sam smothered a smile. He was beginning to find that he liked it when she ordered him about. It made him feel... Well, he wasn't sure, yet. Safe, useful, seen—and something else. Something he couldn't or wouldn't put words to yet. It was all incredibly arousing. "Yes, ma'am."

The glare returned and he couldn't help but admire her eyes, bright with fire. "Don't 'ma'am' me. And get moving! Those sail covers won't remove themselves."

Sam nodded. He had only just learned what a sail cover was, literally the day before, but that didn't matter. He was in Valerie's hands now. Capable, clever, and a little calloused. He doubted there was anything she couldn't do, including teach him to be a competent crew. "Okay. What do you need me to do?"

"Parsons! I need you to trim the jib. Now!" Valerie's hand was on the tiller, while her eyes were locked on the horizon. They were, miraculously, in first place. Well, it wasn't a miracle.

Sam was fast discovering that Kat and Will had spoken the truth when they had described Valerie as the 'best sailor on the island.' Not that he'd really doubted it. The way she handled herself, and the boat, and him—always confident, with a masterful precision. She was knowledgable, not just about the parts of the boat but about the moon and its tides, the hidden rock clusters, the patterns the wind made on the surface of the sea. She was intense, like the sun without shade or the crashing of the white-capped waves. And she didn't hesitate to order him about—not out of insecurity or because she was power-hungry, but because when it came to sailing, Sam was learning, wisdom was not without hierarchy.

Valerie knew what she was doing, knew how to win and how not to lose, knew how to turn Sam into an advantage instead of a good-for-nothing crew. So, he did as he was told. Because that was how he was going to make yesterday up to her; that was how they were going to win. And because, well, listening to her—following her orders, obeying her commands—it felt right and good and natural to him.

"Parsons! Jib sheet, now!" Valerie adjusted the tiller almost imperceptibly. "And I need you to move closer to the bow."

Sam pulled the rope—line, rather—in by a half inch until the narrow triangular sail at the front of the boat stopped billowing. Then he shifted his weight forward, toward the mast, sliding a half-foot down the bench. "That good?"

"Jib's good, but I want your weight even further forward." Valerie scooted up, too, following him until her thigh was pressed against his. "That's better."

It was better. And not just because they had picked up a little speed. It was better because now Sam could feel the warmth of her, filtered through the flimsy fabric of her athletic shorts. He could feel the hard-won muscles in her thigh, tense—and he knew why. "How long until we tack?"

She bit her lip, only taking her eyes off the large red nun ahead of them to glance momentarily at the mainsail above. "Another minute or two. You're going to have to be quick with the jib sheets when you move."

Sam nodded. After a surprisingly successful start—entirely Valerie's effort, with Sam on the stopwatch because Valerie did at least trust him to press buttons and count—they'd been beating upwind for twenty minutes, zigzagging up and across the thorofare. They'd narrowly avoided the Juniper Island ferry and lost some speed in the wake of a busy lobster boat, but they'd managed to secure a spot several boat lengths ahead of Mrs. Wooster and Mrs.

Adams, ahead even of Valerie's coworker, James—Valerie had muttered something about his being "too busy mooning over his girlfriend to sail a Herreshoff with any skill."

Sam supposed there was no place in a race for romance. But that didn't mean he didn't still feel a thrill when Valerie shifted her weight yet again, nudging the exposed skin of his thigh with her splayed knee, or pressed her sweetly curved hip against his, absently. Christ, he felt a thrill, an actual shiver down his spine, every time she opened her mouth to order him about. And once, when he'd looked back in time to see her pink tongue dart out to lick her parted lips—

"Tacking in *ten*, nine, eight, seven—don't loosen that jib sheet yet, Parsons—six, five—you'd better have the other one in hand—four, three, two—okay, get ready to duck your head and move—*now*!"

Valerie shoved the tiller away from her. Sam slid off the bench and crouched in the center of the boat, letting out the starboard sheet with his right hand like they'd practiced and pulling in the port sheet with his left. Behind him, Valerie deftly maneuvered the boat around the nun while switching sides and also letting out the mainsail. Naturally, with her on the tiller, there were no hiccups and not even the threat of a collision.

As they settled onto the bench on the other side of the boat, shifting their weight forward once more, Valerie furrowed her brow.

"What?" Sam cocked his head to the side. "Is something wrong?"

She shook her head. "No, I just... I think you might be a natural."

He laughed, pulling down on the brim of his borrowed hat. "It's only because I have the best teacher."

She said nothing, so he glanced back at her. Valerie's cheeks were pink, and not just because of the salt spray or the whistling wind. Then she shook herself, refocusing on the sailboat. "You've got a kink," she muttered, then took the mainsheet between her teeth and reached, without relinquishing the tiller, across Sam's chest for the jib sheet.

"I've—what?" Sam sucked in his breath as she brushed her arm against his chest, and her long and nimble fingers came curling around his.

Valerie tugged on the jib sheet until it was taut. Her mission accomplished, she removed the mainsheet from her mouth. "A kink, in the line. It wasn't pulling in all the—what did you think I meant?"

Sam flushed. "Nothing. Harding." All he could think about was the white flash of her teeth, biting down hard on the red-flecked mainsheet. That, and the spark that had seemed to jump from her fingers to his, a sensation far beyond static. She was a storm, one he wanted to get stuck in. All fire and fury, fascinating him to no end. He wanted to hear her howl like the wind, watch her hips roll like the thunder, feel her come around him, come alive, come alight—like the lightning that strikes all through the night.

"Are you alright?" She peered at him curiously.

Startled by the sudden intensity of his thoughts, the vivid visualization of his apparently desperate desires, Sam struggled to nod. "I'm—fine."

"You're not seasick, are you?" She preemptively groaned. "Do *not* throw up in the boat. It's hell to clean, and knowing you, you'd probably break something."

Sam tore his eyes from Valerie's lips and opened his own mouth in protest. "I'm not seasick! I'm just... thinking."

She huffed. "I don't need you to think."

His eyes found hers, once more. "Then what do you need me to do?" The wind whistled around them, and the white-caps crashed against the hull.

Valerie swallowed, averting her gaze again. "I need you to let out the jib."

"Are we putting up a spin-whatever?" He'd heard Kat talking about them. Apparently they made the boat go significantly faster.

"No. We are not putting up a spinnaker."

Sam frowned. "Why?" He glanced behind her and saw that they were still in the lead, but James' boat was drawing close.

"Because we're currently on a close reach. You don't put up a spinnaker unless you're running."

"Running?"

"Going directly downwind. A spinnaker is an extra sail, larger and lighter than the jib and the mainsail, that catches additional wind. But it doesn't work unless you're going downwind."

Ah. "So, are we putting one up later?" The course included a downwind leg, Valerie had said.

"No." She sounded sad, rather than angry, and Sam regretted the line of questioning. But then she seemed to swallow her sorrow, and that anger returned. "No, we are not putting up a spinnaker on the next leg, even though we *will* be running."

Sam hesitated, but curiosity won out. "Why not?"

"Because," she ground out, glaring at the mainsail as she let it out a couple inches, "in order for us to put up a spinnaker, we would have to switch places. I would have to go up on the bow and deal with the spinnaker bag, while you took the tiller. And, given that you nearly crashed an Ensign less than twenty-four hours ago, losing me an entire regatta, I don't quite trust you to steer!"

Sam nodded. That was fair enough. "Okay. So, what are we going to do? How are we going to win?"

Valerie pressed her lips together. "We're going wing-to-wing on the downwind leg, after we jibe. And you'll just have to pray that Mrs. Wooster's brand new spinnaker pole snaps in half, or that James is so distracted by Estie that he forgets to secure the halyard. Because, otherwise, we're going to lose this lead."

"I think that went really well!" Sam sounded impressed with her, and himself.

Valerie, who was in the process of climbing out of the rowboat and onto the dinghy float, shot Sam a withering look instead of taking his extended hand. "Because we didn't crash, or lose?"

The Best Crew

He smiled down at her, stepping aside so she had room to stand. "Yeah!"

Steady on her feet, Valerie straightened. It irked her that she had to look up at him still, even when they were standing on the same, flat surface. "We finished third."

He nodded enthusiastically, his gaze bright. "That's good, right? Third place is a bronze medal in the Olympics."

Valerie rolled her eyes and brushed past him on her way to the ramp that led up to the main dock and the clubhouse. "Third place in the Juniper Island August Series is a pair of engraved lowballs."

Sam followed her up the ramp, his footsteps heavy on the stretch of steel. He'd been great ballast, and shockingly good on the sheets, but without a spinnaker on that last leg they might as well have been dead in the water. "Engraved whiskey glasses! Nice!"

"First place," she ground out, glaring at him over her shoulder, "is glory. Victory. A three year streak, for me. And, let's not forget, a giant silver lighthouse that doubles as a cocktail shaker."

Not watching where she was walking, she nearly knocked over a rather frail, elderly man as she stepped off the ramp.

"Oh! I'm so sorry, Mr. Wooster."

He waved away her apology. "No harm, no foul!"

"Also, thank you for taking my great uncle out on your boat, yesterday and today. And my congratulations, to your wife." Valerie tried and failed to keep the bitterness out of her voice.

But Mr. Wooster just smiled fondly. "It's my pleasure. Your Uncle Willie and I have been friends since we were boys, as well you know. He's back at the house with his very kind companion, now. As for Mrs. Wooster's victory, tell her yourself! She's at the tea. And take heart, Valerie. You'll beat her someday."

"I beat her last year, and the year before," Valerie muttered, too low for the old man to hear. "Thank you, Mr. Wooster. We'll go tell her now." She reached behind her for Sam's hand and yanked. "Come on, Parsons. It's tea time."

Stumbling as he caught up to her, Sam appeared a bit bewildered. Had Kat and Will not explained? His next question confirmed it. "Tea time? What is this, Buckingham Palace?"

Valerie sighed and let go of his hand, which was warm and large and—distracting. "It's tradition. Every week, after the series race, there's a tea hosted by a member of the Juniper Island Casino."

"So, like, finger sandwiches? Tea cups? Sugar cubes?"

Valerie nodded grimly. "Yep. And an opportunity for the winner of the race to rub it in my face."

"Oh, come on. They're old ladies. And nice ones, too. They're not going to—"

"Well, well, well..." Mrs. Adams announced gleefully, as they rounded the corner of the clubhouse and came into view. "If it isn't the prodigy." She had taken off her pink visor and was now poised for pleasantries with a porcelain cup of tea.

Mrs. Wooster stood smiling beside her crew, her eyes crinkling behind her sunglasses.

Valerie wished she were as thin as the charts she used to navigate the coastline, so she could slip between the planks of the dock and dissolve into the waiting sea.

"Aren't you going to congratulate me?" Mrs. Wooster's tone was more sly than expectant.

Valerie struggled to say anything, acutely aware of the sun's spotlight and the assembled crowd of windswept racers encircled by their friends and families.

Sam stepped in, smiling as though nothing were wrong. "Mrs. W! Mrs. A! Congratulations on the race today. And what a beautiful spinnaker—I didn't realize they made sails in that color."

It *was* a rather shocking shade of pink.

Mrs. Wooster's smile widened with sincerity. "Why, we had it custom made, to celebrate our friendship!"

Sam shook his head in mock disbelief. "Good sailors and stylish, too! But I wouldn't expect anything less, from two ladies such as you."

Valerie rolled her eyes even as Mrs. Adams sighed. Of course he was flirting with them, again. She didn't know why it annoyed her, but it did. Everything he said and did annoyed her. He was, in a word, annoying.

Suddenly, Sam put his arm around Valerie's shoulders and squeezed. "We'd have joined you in the spinnaker run," he said, as she adjusted to the warmth of his touch and his subtle scent, mingled with sunblock and the ocean's spray. "But Valerie didn't have time to teach me. She's an excellent teacher, did you know?"

Valerie jerked her head back to stare up at him. "What are you—"

He squeezed her shoulders again, and continued, "I mean, as far as sailing goes, she taught me everything I know."

"Which isn't much," she grumbled, resigned to his embrace. Well, it wasn't exactly a hardship. Something about his touch felt... right. She'd noticed it earlier, when her knee had brushed up against his thigh. But she wasn't about to get all wide-eyed and wobbly in the middle of a race.

Sam laughed, as though she'd made a clever joke, and the others joined him. Even James, who was watching from the doorway of the clubhouse, his arm around Estie, chuckled. Love really seemed to loosen some folks up. Valerie felt tight as a sheet in a cleat—caught between the crowd's rock and Sam's hard place. Not that—good lord, she couldn't even master her thoughts.

"Oh, alright, that's enough." Valerie ducked out from under Sam's arm, making an abrupt decision. "We're going."

Sam looked down at her, surprise lighting his blue eyes. "Oh? We're not going to stay for the tea?"

"You *have* to have a cup," piped up Estie from the doorway. "It's delicious!"

"It's tea."

Sam laughed. "Tea's good, Harding. Besides, where have we got to be?"

"Out on the water, while there's still light and wind to spare."

His brow furrowed in confusion. "But the race is over—"

She raised her own eyebrows in challenge. "You said I was a good teacher. Well, it's time for yet another lesson."

Mrs. Wooster narrowed her eyes over her tea cup's rim. "What are you teaching him?"

Sam shifted on his feet to fully face Valerie. "Yeah. What's on the agenda?"

Valerie swallowed as she surveyed all six-foot-three of him. He really was tall. And good-looking. But that wasn't why she was doing this. She was doing this because it was necessary. Necessary, if they wanted to win. And more than anything, Valerie wanted to win. "Spinnakers. Today is the day you learn to set a spinnaker."

Sam's eyes widened. "Really?" He was adorable when he was excited. Like a giant golden retriever.

Valerie nodded, as briskly as she could manage in the face of his eternal sunshine. "Grab a couple of finger sandwiches, Parsons. And maybe a few lemon squares. We'll need provisions." She shook her head, remembering what Uncle Willie had always said. "You can't sail on an empty stomach."

Sam nodded eagerly. "Meet you down on the float in five?"

"Make it two." Valerie stalked off in the direction of the bathroom. Never again. Never again would the two of them lose.

Chapter 6
Spinnaker Lessons

"I can't believe you're making me re-rig this boat. We literally just derigged, less than twenty minutes ago." Sam eyed Valerie, who was sitting in the rowboat's bow, suspiciously. "Was this spinnaker lesson thing a whim?"

Valerie shook her head. "Whims have no place on the water. Instinct, however…"

He continued to row, the muscles in his shoulders rippling as he pulled at the oars with ease. "So, it was a whim."

"It was a calculated decision." She stared out at the empty moorings where, in another couple of hours, the lobster boats would be.

Sam nodded knowingly. "A Hail Mary. Like when you took me on as crew."

Valerie closed her eyes and sighed. "I had no choice, Parsons. Not with you." She opened them again and found him watching her with a certain warmth that, well, she'd be lying if she said she didn't like the way it felt. Flustered, she resolved to return to instructor-mode. A strategic retreat to professionalism, to education-oriented formality. "Now, what do you know about spinnakers?"

"A spinnaker is an extra sail," he parroted her earlier speech.

"Larger and lighter than the jib and the mainsail, it catches additional wind—something to do with its greater surface area and detached rig, I assume."

"Good. That's good."

He smiled. "See? I'm not just a pretty face."

Valerie couldn't help it; she snorted a surprised laugh.

"What? Do you disagree?"

She cocked her head, not trusting herself to speak.

"So you think I *am* just a pretty face?"

Blushing, she shook her head. "That's not what I—"

"Oh? You mean you don't even think that I'm pretty?" He pouted, prettily.

Valerie rolled her eyes. "We both know you're well beyond pretty, Parsons. Now, focus on me, please, and not your reflection in the water. We can't have you metamorphosing before the series is over."

Sam laughed at that, hearty and true. "You've got a good sense of humor, you know that? I mean, it's hidden beneath layers of fury and frustration—all of which, I'm sure, I've earned. But..."

She shot him a look. "But what?"

His blue eyes were warm again, like the waters off the Cape. "You make me laugh, Harding. And I like it. I like you—even when you get all scary-sailor on me." He grinned, glancing up at her through long gold lashes. "*Especially* when you get all scary-sailor on me."

Confused, flustered, and a little aroused, Valerie struggled to come up with a retort. "Just—keep your eyes on the prize, Parsons."

He gazed at her, something hot and heady in his eyes. "Oh, I am."

What? He couldn't mean... "No, I meant—Just don't hit anything."

He sighed, glancing over his shoulder. "Still not letting me live that down, eh? Harding, you're going to have to learn to trust me. I have a sneaking suspicion our standing in the series depends on it."

"I am trusting you," she muttered, and it was partly true. "I'm trusting you to set the spinnaker."

"And you can't do that because...?"

"Because I have to be on the tiller. It's my Uncle Willie's boat, and I'm not letting you, who have the aim and navigational skill of one of my beginner Opti students, steer her." That would be putting their lives, and her great uncle's legacy, in Sam's hands.

Sam nodded, the flirtatious light fading somewhat from his eyes. "Alright, then. Teach me, Valerie. Tell me exactly what to do."

"Did you remember the lemon squares?" Valerie's feet dangled inches above the water below the float. They had finished up the last of their spinnaker runs twenty minutes ago, derigged, and were now watching the sunset from the Abbottville dock—Valerie had directed him there, instead of the Casino, citing the shorter walk back.

Sam fumbled around in his pocket. "Of course. But there were only a few left."

She turned to him, squinting slightly in the evening light. "And you felt bad about taking all of them?"

Sam shook his head firmly. "Not in the slightest." He offered her the squares, which were rather gracelessly wrapped in plastic. "Here."

She huffed a laugh. "I'm impressed. I hadn't pegged you for ruthless."

Twisting his lips, Sam answered honestly. "You seemed like you needed the pick-me-up."

"Oh. Right. Well." Looking away, Valerie bit into a slightly squashed lemon square. Immediately, her eyes rolled back and she let out a long, languid moan.

Sam swallowed. Was that what she sounded like when she—never mind. That wasn't any of his business. Or was it? He'd caught her watching him more than once during the lesson, her eyes dark with—could it be, desire? And there was the way she touched him, without hesitation, guiding his hands as they practiced setting the spinnaker, her fingers lingering on his forearms.

"Sam?" She had finished chewing, and he watched her throat work as she swallowed.

Sam shook himself, meeting her eyes after a long moment. "Uh, yeah?"

"I want more."

So did he. Christ, he wanted all of her. From her wind-wrecked ponytail to the salt-stained tips of her boat shoes. From her dark eyes, always ready to roll, to her lightly calloused fingertips. From her anger to her pleasure, again and again and again. "More?" He could give her more. He could give her—

"Lemon squares," she said with a shake of her head, as though it were obvious. And, he supposed, it had been obvious. He was just too deeply in her thrall to pay attention to anything any more, anything at all. With the exception of her, of course. The curve of her ear, her furrowed brow, the inches that separated them, that exquisite frown. He wanted to tease a smile from those lips. He wanted to work for it. Work, and work, and work, until they were both sweaty and senseless.

"Sam?"

"Yes! Of course." He handed her the rest of the squares.

She opened her mouth to bite into another, and then seemed to remember herself. "Do you want one?" She offered him the small pile.

Sam shook his head. "No, I—" What could he say? What excuse could he possibly have? Honesty sounded too creepy: "No, thanks. I'm enjoying watching you eat them too much to have one myself?" He would sound insane. And scary. Like some kind of stalker. Seriously, he had to get grip.

"Alright, then." Valerie shrugged, apparently oblivious to his internal turmoil. "More for me." Then she shoved a whole one in her mouth. Goddamnit, she was glorious.

Sam swallowed. "Should we, uh, head up?"

Valerie continued to chew. "Up?"

"To Abbottville."

She nodded, swallowing. "Yeah, we might as well. It's almost time for dinner and I promised Will and Kat I'd have you back for that."

Sam frowned. "When did you see them?"

"At the tea, while you were getting finger sandwiches and lemon squares, and flirting with much older, not to mention married, women."

He laughed, and she raised an eyebrow, challenging him to protest. "Oh, alright. I did flirt a bit more with Mrs. Wooster and Mrs. Adams. But it's all part of my strategy!"

"Oh?" She pushed up from the float. "And what's that? To make me jealous?"

Sam, who was in the process of rising himself, tripped and nearly fell into the water. "What?"

"It was a joke, Parsons. I'm not jealous of a couple of old ladies. That would require my being interested in you."

Her words knocked the wind out of his figurative sails. "Right. Because that's never going to happen."

She bit her lip, looking almost as uncomfortable as he felt. As well as a bit... guilty? She turned away from the sunset, from him as well, and started walking toward the ramp. "So, what's the strategy?"

"The strategy?" Sam scrambled to keep up.

"Don't run on the dock, Parsons. And yeah, why are you flirting with women who could be your grandmothers?"

"I'm trying to throw them off their game, obviously."

Valerie marched up the metal ramp, which rattled beneath both of their weights. "And here I thought you just had a thing for older women."

"Age doesn't factor into it, for me." Sam rushed to add, "I mean, I'm not—legality, of course, is something I consider."

Valerie laughed, then, a true and beautiful sound that seemed to echo across the empty dock and the rocks below and the now still waters of the thorofare that surrounded them. "Relax, Parsons. I know you're not a creep."

He exhaled in relief.

"Hurry up." She strode across the narrow pier that connected the ramp to the land. "Honestly, with those legs, you ought to be faster than me."

"What's the rush?" Sam was enjoying himself, enjoying Valerie's company. As much as he loved his friends, he didn't want this one-on-one time to end.

Apparently of a different mind, Valerie walked faster. "I'm hungry."

Sam lengthened his strides as they crossed onto the compound's front lawn. "You're welcome to come to dinner with me and the twins."

Valerie shook her head, making a sharp left turn towards Widow's Woods. "Send those fools my love. I've got a book waiting for me."

"Right!" Sam stopped before he walked into a flowerbed. "Kat said you're a big reader. Romance novels, yeah?"

Valerie spun around, backlit by the setting sun. "And what about it?" She sounded... defensive. Her hackles were once again raised.

Sam smiled, shaking his head. "Nothing. I've just never read a romance. And I've got a lot of free time, this month. Do you think... Would you maybe recommend one?"

Excitement lit Valerie's brown eyes. "Seriously?"

"Yeah, why not?"

She clapped her hands together, grinning. It was quite the transformation, compared to her earlier stern-faced sailor. "Historical or contemporary?"

Sam thought for a moment. "Contemporary?"

"Do you care about the genders of the main characters?"

He shook his head, thinking of his own flexibility on that front.

"Comedic or dramatic?"

"A little bit of both?"

She nodded, growing pensive. "Any triggers I should be aware of?"

"No, I don't think so. But no deaths, please."

"What about zombies?"

Sam laughed, but it appeared Valerie was serious. "Oh, I'd rather not read anything too gruesome or overly magical, to start."

"Right, got it." She bit her lip, and Sam longed to—"I'll think about it tonight and get back to you tomorrow."

"Thank you. I—"

"Don't thank me yet," she said, smiling. Sam's heart stuttered at the sight. "Thank me when you've fallen in love with a new genre." Then she spun back around and practically flounced off in the direction of the woods.

Sam watched Valerie walk away with wide eyes. What a change had come over her, during their conversation. He was in awe of her enthusiasm, her excitement, her eagerness. He wanted to explore her, body and soul. Learn her, inside and out. Know her, and not just as a crew knows his skipper.

"Samwise!" Will was walking down the sloping lawn toward him. "How was it?"

Amazing. Breathtaking. Brilliant. Exhilarating. Occasionally erotic. Sam struggled to contain the sudden surge of feelings that threatened to spill over and out. "It was fun!"

"I hope Valerie didn't give you too hard of a time." Will frowned. "She's a wonderful person, but slightly scary on the sea."

Sam shook his head. "No, she's not. She's smart, and sensible. She knows what she's doing, that's all. We would've won if she could have trusted me with the tiller."

Will nodded sagely. "Yes, she should have trusted you."

"No! That's not what I meant. She was right not to trust me, before. I ruined her race yesterday. But now…" She trusted him, after a whole day on the water and some much needed guidance. Valerie trusted Sam. And it felt so good, so right, so… "We're going to win the series, Will." He'd learn to sail, for Valerie. He'd learn to sail so well, they'd win. For Valerie, he'd do anything.

Chapter 7
Boat Picnic

"Knock knock!" Kat's voice echoed through the Cliff House on Sunday morning.

Valerie reluctantly set aside her novel. "What is it, Kat?"

Her cousin stepped into the living room, Will and Sam in tow. When Sam's eyes met hers, Valerie couldn't help but shiver. There was an intensity there, born of a not unwelcome interest. "We're going on a boat picnic and you're coming with us." Kat folded her arms across her chest; she would brook no protest.

Valerie protested anyway. "But I'm reading."

"You can read on the boat and the beach."

"But it's my day off."

"And what better way to spend it?"

"But I don't want to."

"We both know that's utter bullshit."

It was. It was utter bullshit. Kat was right, on all counts, but Valerie had had to argue. It was in her nature. Sam hadn't seemed to mind yesterday. Sam, who would also be going on this boat picnic... "Oh, alright."

Kat smirked triumphantly. "Go change. We'll be down at the

dock. Don't worry about lunch—we've got leftover lobster and champagne from the old cellar."

Valerie stood, collecting her book. "And water?"

Kat laughed. "Yes, of course. And Will's designated driver on the way back, so don't even think about trying to stay sober."

Ten minutes later, Valerie met her cousins and Sam down at the Abbottville dock with something akin to butterflies in her belly. The tide was high and the ramp was practically horizontal. As she strode down it, Sam looked up from the picnic bags and smiled. He really was a ray of sunshine. And it was a startlingly bright day.

"Does anyone have any sunblock?"

Will poked his head out from beneath the motorboat's canvas canopy. "Of course. Thirty and seventy-five SPF. Did you forget?"

Valerie nodded, stepping forward to accept the bottle her cousin offered. "Thanks."

"Do you want any help with that?" Sam was watching her, his lower lip between his teeth. Valerie was mesmerized, momentarily. "Harding?"

"Are you two really going to call each other by your last names for the rest of time?" Kat started the boat's engine. "We're going on a boat picnic, for crying out loud. Let loose! Oh, and get in, will you? Valerie, you can apply your sunblock on the way."

Obediently, Sam carried the picnic bags onto the boat, placing them on its floor before turning back to take Valerie's small tote. "What's in this?" He laughed. "Rocks?"

Valerie couldn't help it. She smiled back. "No, that would be Will's bag."

"He collects them still, does he?"

Valerie nodded. "It drives his mother up the wall."

Sam chuckled, shaking his head. "What's your poison, then? Books?"

She shot him a finger-gun, and then immediately regretted it. "You know it."

He just smiled. "Did you by any chance bring one for me?"

His sustained interest pleased her. "Give me a second. I've gotta cast us off."

"Need a hand?" He had one foot in the boat and the other on the float.

Untwisting the sternline from the furthest cleat, Valerie shook her head. "I'll just be a second." She walked to the bow, undoing the knot there, as well. Then she gave the boat a push, jumping in just as it started to drift away from the dock. Kat revved the engine once Valerie was safely in the boat, and they were off.

"Where are we going?" Valerie called over the sound of the motor. In the rush to get ready, she'd forgotten to ask.

Sam shrugged, pulling the last of the fenders into the boat. Will, who was watching for seals and porpoises, ignored the question or—more likely—didn't even hear it. Setting down her soda in the boat's cup holder, Kat answered at last, "Blackstone."

"That's a forty minute one way trip!"

Kat scoffed. "You brought a book, didn't you?"

As per usual, Valerie had brought several. Speaking of which... "Sam, I've got your book, if you want it." She sat on the bench in the front, under the green canvas canopy, and fished around in her bag for the stack of paperbacks.

He walked slowly from the stern to the bow, tiptoeing behind Will before ducking under the canopy's shelter. "Thanks! But do you want me to help you with your sunscreen, first? I don't know how quickly you burn, but—"

"I don't need your help."

He raised his eyebrows. "Are you planning on wearing that shirt the whole time?"

Valerie glanced down at the faded button down, once her mother's, which she now used as a cover up. "No."

"Then you need to do your back."

"I *know*. I can apply my own sunblock, Parsons. I've been doing it for twenty-six years."

He nodded, raising his hands in submission. "Okay. Doubtful

that you applied your own sunblock when you were a baby. But, regardless, I'm just saying, you don't have to now. I can help you."

"Like you helped me win yesterday?" She regretted the words, immediately. But Sam didn't wince. He only smiled, self-deprecatingly.

"Okay, so maybe I'm not the best crew. But I can see if you miss a spot. Or two."

The boat slammed into some wake. Will yelped in protest as Kat poked her head out from behind the control panel, looking distinctly unapologetic. "Sorry! The Barclays were really booking it in their HBI. Carry on with your argument!"

There was no way Kat could hear them over the wind, which meant Valerie was simply being predictable in her hostility. She sighed. "Oh, alright. You can get my back. But I've still got the rest of my body to do, so I don't need your help just yet." She handed him a book. "Try that. Elizabeth Brooks is one of my favorites, and not just because I know her personally."

Sam accepted the worn paperback copy of *Ski Bum*. "Thanks! I'll dig right in, then. Give a shout when you need me."

Except that Sam didn't dig right in. He certainly opened the book, and flipped the page a couple times, but his eyes never left her for more than a moment. Valerie supposed he thought he was being sly. Or maybe he wasn't even aware of his actions. He looked so eager, so hungry, so... awed—and by her.

Valerie knew she was fairly pretty, and she had an athletic body. But Sam Parsons stared at her like she was the sun and he wanted to stop her from ever setting. As she lathered up her arms and legs, Valerie allowed herself to imagine, just imagine, what his touch might feel like. In a moment, she realized with a start, she'd know.

Valerie cleared her throat. "I'm going to—I'm taking this off now." She started to unbutton the old shirt, and Sam's eyes widened. It wasn't like she was wearing nothing beneath it. But still, her heart beat faster with aroused excitement. Her hands a bit shaky, she tossed him the SPF thirty. "Would you?" Then she slipped the shirt off her shoulders and let it fall, fluttering, to her feet.

Sam nodded. "Of—of course." His voice was husky, as if from desire or disuse. Certainly not the latter. But the former—could it be? She supposed she knew he wanted her, but... how badly?

Sam squirted some sunblock into his palm and warmed it between his hands. "Could you turn around, please?"

Valerie nodded, shifting in her seat. She wished she could watch this. She wished she could see. In lieu of a better view, however, she allowed her eyes to flutter closed. Until he touched her. And then her eyes were open wide. It was electric between them, like a wire that had suddenly gone live. Valerie couldn't help but gasp softly as Sam smoothed the lotion over the skin between her shoulder blades.

He cleared his throat. "Sorry. I know it's cold."

She shook her head, not wanting him to stop. "No, no—I—It's fine. Keep going." Belatedly, she added, "Please."

He laughed softly. "Please? I think you like ordering me about, Harding. With or without niceties." And then his hands were stroking her shoulders, cupping the back of her neck, sliding along the back strap of her bikini—and under, "Just so there aren't any lines."

The sensual onslaught continued for what felt like an eternity. But eventually, his hands slowed, lingering against her slightly sticky skin. "There," he murmured, and she wanted to protest. But what? He'd done what she'd asked him to do. It was over. If she wanted him to touch her more, she'd need a better excuse. Or maybe... the truth?

"Sam, I—"

"Oy, lovebirds!" Kat had a keen eye and truly terrible timing. "Change of plans. Let's go to White Whale's Cove."

Sam cocked his head. "Like... the titular monster in *Moby Dick*? You people really have a thing for him."

Valerie picked up her cover up from the floor, where it had been lying in a lump, quite forgotten. "No, it was named before the book came out. And I don't know if I'd agree that that whale was monster.

Not more of a monster than Ahab, at least. Anyway, there used to be a whale's skeleton along the beach, but some alums from Brixley—you know, the boarding school where they all look like they just stepped out of a J. Crew catalog?"

"That's all boarding schools," Kat interjected.

Valerie inclined her head, continuing, "They decided they wanted to hang it in the stairwell at the center of their science building. Anyway, the cove is just one beach on Gulls Island."

"The best beach. And it looks empty, which is shocking considering it's a Sunday." Kat slowed the boat. "All in favor?"

Valerie and Sam both returned an "aye." Will, who was still watching for sea creatures, said nothing.

"White Whale's Cove it is!" Kat announced, steering the boat to port.

Valerie eyed Sam surreptitiously. "Thank you," she said, when he turned and caught her staring. "I could have done it myself but—"

"But you didn't have to," he finished her sentence for her, not the way she would have done, but she supposed he wasn't wrong. It was nice, she was starting to discover, this whole counting-on-someone thing. Sam was (shockingly) a good crew, and a good—friend? No, that wasn't right, not when he made her heart beat fast and her thighs squeeze together so tight.

Gulping down the briny air, Valerie realized she didn't quite know what to think—or what to do. Still, she'd learned long ago that it was better to act in all honesty than to hide the truth or lie about it.

Sam jumped down into the icy water as Kat lifted the still engine, relishing the sudden chill. He needed it. Things had gotten entirely too hot under that green canvas canopy. Well, he wasn't complaining. He just wished they hadn't been at sea with his friends, Valerie's cousins. It made his growing arousal all the more awkward. Hence his volunteering to be the first one in the frigid water, anchor in hand, as he pulled the boat closer to dry land.

"What about here?" He called out to Kat, pointing to a cluster of large rocks. "Can I wedge the anchor under these?"

She nodded. "Just make sure it'll hold." Then, the engine off and in the air, she started toward the front of the boat, where Valerie was gathering the large canvas totes and the one cooler bag that contained several bottles of champagne they'd stolen from the Abbottville cellar.

Sam successfully wedged the anchor under and between the rocks, tugging on the rope to make sure it wouldn't dislodge if the beach met with any waves over the course of their stay. Pleased with himself, and increasingly numb to the water's cold, he waded back to the boat. "Here, toss me a bag or two."

Valerie nodded, handing him two totes filled with towels and sandwiches. "Hold them high above the water," she added, but her commanding tone faltered as her fingers brushed against his exposed wrist.

Sam grinned. "We wouldn't want them getting wet, now, would we?"

"Sam, get your mind out of the gutter." Kat emerged from under the canopy, throwing one leg over the side of the boat and sliding into the water. "Valerie, can you pass me the champagne? Precious cargo, you know."

Tearing his eyes from Valerie, who was rolling her eyes in an attempt to suppress a smile, Sam strode away in the direction of the beach. He set the bags down in a comfortable looking spot—well, as comfortable as he could achieve, considering the beach wasn't sand but rock.

"You don't need my permission, you know." Kat set the champagne-filled cooler bag down on the dried seaweed that marked the high tide line. "In fact, I'll give you my blessing."

Sam's first instinct was to feign ignorance. "What?"

"Don't play dumb. I've seen the way you look at her. And you've done more than look at her."

That specific allegation threw him for a loop, however. "What are you talking about?"

Kat leveled him with a disbelieving look. "Valerie!"

"No. I mean, obviously. But I haven't—We haven't—What are you talking about?"

His oldest friend let out a knowing chuckled, reminding him that she'd always been able to see right through him. "You didn't offer to help *me* with my sunblock."

Sam blanched. "Uh... Do you need help with your sunblock?"

"No, doofus. I already applied. Besides, I don't want to inspire any jealousy." She smirked, and he knew that protest would be pointless. Besides, he considered as he watched Valerie trudge ashore, Kat's blessing had been something he'd been hoping for. Not that he'd really dared to imagine, until today, that things would ever go that way. But it had been fun to flirt with Valerie, if he had only indulged in the activity slightly. Even more fun to see her seethe and snap, when he flirted with old ladies—when the old ladies flirted back. And if Kat was right—if Valerie was into it, too—he might as well make a move.

Kat reached for the champagne. "Come on, let's get one of these bad boys open."

Sam nodded, not taking his eyes off of the woman in the worn button down. As she approached, she swung the tote bag off her shoulder and glanced up, meeting his gaze. Sam rather thought he could have looked into those wide, brown eyes for days. She slowed in silent answer, showing no signs of wanting to look away. The two of them seemed to be stuck in a sort of trance, heady and high. But, like gulls on a pier, they were both startled back into reality as the champagne went off with a sudden *pop* and a subsequent fizz.

"That wake we hit must have really shaken it," Kat concluded before she quickly brought the bottle to her lips to catch the foam. Spluttering, she pulled back. "Oh, christ. It's up my nose." She held the overflowing bottle out to Sam, who had reluctantly torn his gaze from Valerie to observe his friend's antics. "Take it, will you?"

Sam grasped the elegantly curved and faintly dusty bottle by the neck, and took a deep draught. The fizz caught him, too, and he coughed. Beside him, he heard the crunch of Valerie's boat shoes against the sharp stones and fragmented mussel shells that made up the rocky beach. And then he heard something far sweeter still than the sound of her approaching step: her laughter, like honey and wine —champagne rather, dug up from some deep cellar. How rare the sound, and welcome. A delicacy. And yet, not delicate.

"You're both fools," she announced, setting down her bag. She reached for the bottle, then, her fingers curling around Sam's. A gesture like that, it couldn't have been a mistake. "Let me show you how it's done."

Sam saw that her eyes were bright with amusement, and a spark of that same arrogance that she'd earned, year after year, race after race, working hard to win—even when stuck with a crew who couldn't tell tiller from telltale. But this wasn't the sailor he was seeing, though he could feel the slight calluses on her fingers from a summer of working the sheets.

This was another side of Valerie, playful and proud. Sam was getting a glimpse of the woman within, the one who read romances and wasn't afraid of ghosts; the one who could hold her liquor better than her cousins, according to Kat, despite their being older; the one who wrangled countless students year round and a single clueless crew on Saturdays now.

Christ, but how he liked to be wrangled by Valerie. To be ordered about, to be commanded, to be given the chance to learn as well as earn her trust, however long it took. Sam lived for the opportunity to do what she told him to. To try, again and again until he got it right, to make her happy. To help her win.

But he wondered—in moments like this when their hands were practically intertwined, or when their thighs were pressed up against each other as they sat in the sailboat side by side, or when his fingers lingered on the smooth skin between her shoulder blades as he helped her apply—he wondered if there were other things he could try. Other ways to make her happy, other victories they could work toward, together.

The corner of her mouth kicked up. "Let go of the bottle, Parsons."

He obeyed her cool command instantly. And watched, with bated breath, as Valerie brought the bottle to her licked and parted lips. She tilted her head back, slowly, torturously, exposing her lightly tanned throat—and letting the champagne flow into her open mouth. Like water, after a long drought.

For a moment, Sam wished—inanely, insanely—that he were a mere bubble in the brew, so that he might have the taste of her, sweet like a lemon square and tart as the ancient wine; so that he might know the feel of her, soft and ripe and velvet as the star-spangled night.

Valerie swallowed and Sam clumsily followed suit, gulping down the salty air. The sultry, sexy, sensual woman in front of him didn't splutter, or cough, or complain about the fizz having found its way up into her nostrils. She simply smirked. "And that's how it's done."

Mesmerized, Sam nodded.

Valerie offered him the bottle. "Want to try again?"

Sam licked his own lips, nodding eagerly. "Please."

Something daring and delightful sparked in Valerie's dark eyes. "Well, since you asked nicely..." She handed him the champagne and he quickly pressed his lips to the rim, precisely where her own had been—as if he could catch the ghost of her there, keep some piece of her with him forever.

But there was no relic, no remnant of her, beyond the knowledge he would always treasure that their lips had touched by proxy. And Sam knew, and ached in knowing, that that would never be enough. He wanted Valerie, all of Valerie. He would never settle for a mere proxy. Not if there was even the slightest chance that she wanted him, too.

Chapter 8
The Pool

"So, I assume Lasers have spinnakers, too?"

Valerie huffed a laugh as she stepped onto the ramp leading down to the Casino's designated Laser float. "No, they have enough sail as it is. Seventy-six square feet of it, to be precise."

Pulleys rattled and clinked as Sam hefted the detached mast he was carrying a little higher on his shoulder; Valerie caught a glimpse of his muscles flexing out of the corner of her eye. "If they don't have spinnakers, what's the point of this exercise? Shouldn't we be focused on Herreshoffs?"

Valerie stepped off the ramp and onto the float, setting her own mast to rest against the wooden planks between the white fiberglass hulls. "Lasers are simple boats, low to the water and governed by a single sail. One sail, one sheet. Standard tiller and rudder arrangment. No keel, just a dagger board whose depth you control."

Sam placed his mast delicately beside hers, straightening to squint at her with no small amount of skepticism. "In summary, they're completely different from the kind of boat that you've been teaching me how to sail."

Valerie inclined her head.

"Again, how is this going to help? Don't get me wrong, I'm all for an afternoon cruise with you, especially if Lasers are as easy to sail as you say—"

Blushing slightly at his eagerness to spend time with her, she nevertheless raised a hand, wagging one finger. "Whoa, there, Parsons. I never said easy." She shook her head, suppressing a smile at his arrogance. The man had been on the water for a week, exactly. The last thing he needed was to get cocky. "Lasers are sensitive to your every movement. If your hand, the one that's holding the tiller, twitches... If your fingers, pinching the sheet, relax their grip... If you're uncomfortable and decide to shift in your seat..."

"I just can't win," he concluded with an air of defeat.

"Don't say that," she chided, playfully. "You're my crew. If you can't win, I can't win. You don't want me to lose, do you?"

He lifted his head sharply to look at her with the same intensity as he'd possessed when he'd watched her sip champagne straight from the bottle on the beach almost a week prior. His voice was low when he answered, and she felt it deep in her core. "No. I want you to win. I want *us* to win."

Valerie swallowed, hitherto dormant butterflies in her stomach fluttering at the idea that together they were more than the sum of their individual selves. "Right. Well, if you want *us* to win, *you* have to understand that sailing is a set of transferable skills. Yes, every boat is different. And most people stick to one or two classes of sailboats, one or two particular vessels, in order to hone their skills and perfect their racing. But the true test of a sailor is not their performance in a boat they know well because it's what they've always sailed. It's whether or not they can adapt—to the wind, to the water, to a new make and model, to whatever."

"But I'm still learning," Sam protested, his blue eyes wide beneath the brim of her great uncle's hat. "I don't even have a handle on Herreshoffs—"

Valerie nodded. "Exactly. You're still malleable. Which is why I think this will help."

He narrowed his eyes at her. "How?"

Valerie didn't even try not to roll her eyes. "I could lecture you about it on the dock all day, or we could go out on the water and you could see for yourself. But the wind won't last all afternoon…"

He lifted the hat, running a large yet elegant hand through his wheat-blond hair before replacing it on his head. "Alright, alright. Just tell me what to do to get this thing rigged."

Valerie laughed, loud and clear, and the sound washed over Sam a wave gently breaking.

He turned his head to squint in her direction, careful not to shift his weight in the process. "Why are you laughing? Have I done something profoundly stupid?"

She shook her head and called out over the water to him, "No! You're perfect, if a little rigid."

Perfect, eh?

As if she could read his mind, she shook her head and—to his surprise and delight—laughed again. "Remember to relax, Parsons. Roll with the punches."

"What punches?"

He couldn't quite see her roll her eyes, but he could hear it in the way she answered him—not without a certain fondness, though, he was pleased to note. "It's a metaphor."

Sam pulled in his mainsail a quarter of an inch, even as he adjusted the tiller to compensate for the closer haul. "For what?"

"Life, the universe, and everything!" She sounded free as a bird, glorious in its flight. "Do you see those islands over there?"

Ducking below the sail so he could see, Sam strained his eyes, searching for islands against the opposite shoreline. He pitched his voice above the wind, "You mean those little clusters of rock?" One was decorated with two pine trees, but the rest were barren and craggy and dotted with white gulls.

Valerie nodded, her face turned up to inspect her sail as she shouted, "I'm going to tack in a few seconds, after you, then we can cross the thorofare on a reach. Those rocks are remnants of the old quarries. Behind them is what we call the swimming pool."

Nodding, Sam pushed the tiller toward the sail. "Tacking!" He ducked, passed the sheet between his hands, and settled on the other side of the boat even as the boom crossed overhead. Valerie hadn't been lying; Lasers were both shockingly simple and surprisingly sensitive. He'd nearly capsized twice, and not because he hadn't been paying attention. Although, it was a little hard to focus when Valerie was near.

She followed suit, decidedly more gracefully. "Keep an eye out for fancy motor boats," she warned him, once she was seated. "They tend to bulldoze through, with no regard for the speed limit."

Sam nodded, his attention split hopelessly between his sail, their destination, and Valerie, who was a fair bit closer to him than she had been. He didn't even have to yell, when he inquired after the so-called pool. "Has it got a diving board?"

She huffed a laugh, shaking her head. "Hardly. It's an old quarry, filled with a half century of rainwater. We'll beach our Lasers on Sheep Island and hike through the pine forest to get to it. Don't worry, it's not far."

True to Valerie's vision, they sailed their Lasers into a little cove, hopped out into the icy water, and half-dragged, half-lifted the narrow boats onto the beach. Only once their sterns were well past the high tide line, marked by washed up, sun-dried seaweed, did Valerie seem satisfied. "Shall we?"

"Happily," Sam replied, returning her a cheeky smile. He was rewarded with her faint blush—which deepened when he asked the question, "But what are we going to swim *in*?"

"Oh." Her lips were round, the color of ripening raspberries. "I completely forgot about bathing suits."

Sam shrugged, willing his body to settle down. "I'm comfortable going commando."

Valerie leveled him with a look. "Commando is when you're

The Best Crew

clothed, with the exception of your underwear. I think you mean 'nude.'"

Sam grinned, even as his heart skipped a beat. "You said it, not me."

Rolling her eyes, she set off toward a little path between the trees at the edge of the beach. "It's a public quarry, Parsons. There could be children there! You are *not* swimming in the nude."

"Your loss, captain..."

She was silent for a moment and, although he couldn't see her face, he would have sworn before a court of law that she was fighting a smile when she muttered, "Shut up, crew."

In the end, after they had trekked up a sloping hill and through a small but dense pine wood, they found the quarry to be deserted.

Sam marveled at the sight, a massive chunk taken out of the earth. Its edges were straight and their angles square—manmade, softened only slightly by the elements. The water was clean and clear, still yet sparkling in the afternoon sun.

Immediately, he began to undress. First, he tossed his hat to the ground, then he pulled his shirt over his head. As he let it fall, fluttering, to the pine-needled floor, he caught sight of Valerie. She was staring at him, a nervous look in her eye. Curious, given the confidence she'd displayed during their boat picnic. "Relax, Harding. I'm not taking off my boxers." He did, however, shimmy out of his shorts.

She exhaled, nodding, but her eyes were trained on his torso. Not so subtly, Sam gave a flex. Instantly, her gaze jumped up to meet his.

"See anything you like?" He smirked at her widening eyes.

But then her lips twitched. "Maybe," she conceded, to Sam's surprise. "Tell me, are those abdominals from work or for show?"

She'd tossed a gauntlet to the ground, and Sam wasn't about to let it lie there, neglected. "I'll show you," he murmured, smirking, then launched himself over the edge of the quarry.

Sam hit the water with a significant splash. It was warm, to his surprise, and slightly sweet. Rainwater, indeed. He pushed a hand through his sopping hair, treading water as he looked up at Valerie. "Aren't you going to join me?"

Her eyes sparkled and without warning she started to strip. Off went her t-shirt, revealing a blue sports bra. Her athletic shorts stayed on, to Sam's disappointment, as he was left wondering about the cut of her panties.

"Move over, Parsons!"

He shook himself. "What?"

Valerie took a few steps back from the edge. "I said, *move*."

Dutifully, he swam a few lengths to the left. Valerie, meanwhile, took a running leap off the edge of the quarry and landed in the water with even less grace than he had. She surfaced a few seconds later like some freshwater selkie, her hair dark and wet. After a moment of sun-drenched basking, her eyes fluttered open.

"Nice cannonball," Sam called to her, when he had recovered from the sight of her. "But I bet you can't do a flip."

One brow arched, Valerie then disappeared underwater. A moment later, Sam felt her grab his ankle and yank. He went under, spluttering at first and then searching for her in the darkness—but she was gone and when he surfaced he found her a few feet away, treading water with a look of amused disdain. "I can do anything you can do."

He stared in stunned silence at her brazen beauty.

Valerie's tongue darted out to catch a stray droplet from the curve of her glistening lips.

Sam wondered at her words, at their unwitting promise. If he kissed her now, would she kiss him back?

A hoot and a holler from the far side of the quarry broke the spell that had momentarily seized Sam—and, he rather thought, Valerie. In unison, they turned their heads toward the growing cacophony. A group of teenagers had gathered on the distant edge and were now tossing pool floats into the water and preparing to join them.

Sam turned back to Valerie, whose wet hair was dark as night and shining in the bright sunlight. "Do you want to get out of here?"

She glanced at him. "Not keen to share?"

Not you. Never you. "I like being able to hear what my skipper has to say, and with the racket they're making..."

Valerie's lips twitched and she jerked her head in the direction of the quarry wall, which had been cut into a kind of uneven stair. "Come on, I know a place."

Sam grinned and swam after her. "Why do I get the feeling I'm not the first man you've said that to?"

She didn't dignify that with a glance over her shoulder, but she did respond coolly, "Because I'm twenty-six, not sixteen. If you're expecting virginity or chastity from me... Well, you're barking up the wrong tree, or maybe you were born in the wrong century."

Sam laughed so hard he struggled to swim. When at last he had caught his breath—just in time to lose it again, as Valerie gracefully pulled herself out of the water, her lean muscles flexing with power and promise—he cocked his head to one side. "Does that make this a date, then?"

Valerie turned and placed her hands on her hips as she stood high above him. Her expression was a curious mix—she was somehow both flustered by him and haughtily imperious. "Nonsense, Parsons."

"You were the one who insinuated romance. Well, sex, I suppose."

"In response to your implication!" She shook her head, but couldn't seem to keep her lips from curving. "Now, be a good crew and do what your skipper tells you to do."

Her words stirred something deep in his soul. His cock, too, twitched, and his arousal imbued his next words with a sensuality that overrode their intended playfulness. "And what is that, o captain, my captain?"

Valerie watched him for a long moment, her eyebrows arched with a kind of erotic authority. "Get your ass out of the water."

Sam grinned and made a show of hoisting himself onto mostly dry rock. Her eyes followed him, widening slightly as he flexed his arms, as he brought himself out of the water to kneel at her pale feet. "My ass, eh? I thought you were more interested in my abs."

Valerie's gaze met his, her eyes dark with desire, but she said nothing. Sam slowly—carefully, lest he slip on the slick granite—stood. Their faces were inches apart, and he could feel the warm puffs of air from her parted lips. Sam's gaze flickered away from her eyes, breaking their contact for one brief moment, to look at those pretty pink lips. Automatically, his tongue darted out to moisten his own lips, in preparation for a well-craved kiss.

As he bent his head down a fraction of an inch, her arms rose—to caress his shoulders, he assumed, or perhaps to cling to his damp neck. Either way, Sam's eyes fluttered shut and he leaned in for the kiss that would change everything, the kiss that would alter the course of his life—but it never came.

Instead, he heard Valerie giggle. And then her hands, which had indeed settled on his shoulders, gave a little shove. Sam found himself stumbling, tumbling backwards, his arms flailing and his eyes opening wide to take in the cloudless sky—before he crashed back into the quarry and a half century of rainwater closed over his head.

Even before he surfaced, he could hear the sound of her laughter, like sunlight filtering through the water, warm and bright—and stronger than the darkness that shadowed the hewn depths of the quarry. And at the sound, Sam couldn't help but smile.

Chapter 9
The Second Race

"Settle down, Parsons."

Sam ceased tapping Will's boat shoes, which he'd borrowed for the duration of the series, against the wooden slats. "Sorry," he murmured, glancing at his skipper—the cool, calm, and collected woman who held the tiller.

"You're nervous," she observed, eyeing him momentarily before returning her gaze to the starting line. There, between the committee boat and a government buoy, eleven boats were clustered. They were stationary, as stationary as any boat could be, because—Valerie had explained this—they were in irons, their sails flapping uselessly as they faced directly and deliberately into the wind. In a minute and a half, when the start sounded, each boat would dip its bow a couple degrees below its current position and, catching the wind, start to move forward again.

Valerie had assured Sam this kind of delaying tactic was a standard way to start. She, however, had had a different idea: harness a distant puff of wind in order to swoop in below the committee boat at the last minute, cross the line with maximum momentum, and steal the other boats' wind just as they began to beat their way up to the first mark.

"Don't you trust me?" Her eyes met his and he struggled to hear her over his own heartbeat. "I'm telling you, it's a good strategy."

Swallowing, Sam nodded once. "I trust you." Of course he trusted her. He trusted her more than anyone he'd ever known before. And he felt like, if he could just *tell* her—but now was not the time for revelations.

Valerie adjusted the mainsheet, her expression stern yet not without warmth. "Then what's wrong?"

The horn blew briefly, signaling a minute until the start. Automatically, Sam confirmed the time on the trusted stopwatch that Valerie's great uncle had bequeathed to her. "Nothing," he said with a shake of his head. Nothing was wrong. But nothing was right, either. Now that he knew that he wanted her, wanted all of her, wanted no one and nothing but her—each and every one of her exasperated eye rolls, and the way she snorted when she succumbed at last to her own laughter, and the curve of her lips that had had him on his knees, craving her kiss—he couldn't focus. "I'm just antsy."

Valerie frowned. "Yeah, I can tell. You're quiet. And you're not... yourself." She shrugged when he narrowed his eyes. "You know. All teasing and tempting and what not."

Sam cocked his head. Tempting?

"Oh, don't give me that look. We've already addressed the fact that you're very attractive. And, usually, a reservoir of good humor." She twisted her lips thoughtfully. "Did you have enough to eat?"

Tearing his eyes away from her lips, which were pursed as though in prelude to a kiss—reminding him of what had almost been, before she pushed him in—he shook his head. "It's not my stomach."

Her gaze darted to the mainsail, which she subsequently trimmed. "And you're not seasick."

"As I said, it's not my stomach."

She glanced at him again, her eyes dark. The breeze picked up, tugging tendrils of her chestnut hair free from the confines of her ponytail. How he ached to lift his hand, to brush behind her ear each and every errant strand. And he almost did just that—but then the horn blew again, three times.

"Thirty seconds," he announced, although she already knew. Her eyes were on the starting line.

"We can talk about it later," she said, distracted by what actually mattered: the race. It was, after all, the only reason he was here in this boat with her. Or at least it had been. He hadn't planned this proximity, hadn't craved this contact. Not at first. At first, he'd simply felt bad. And he'd been looking for something to fill his days. And she'd seemed... Oh, Sam didn't know. Not like a puzzle, to be solved, or a code, to be cracked. Just like a person, to be appreciated. And, maybe, if he spent some time with her, understood.

Because he had felt, from the start, a desire to understand her better. To know her—not biblically, but certainly more intimately. He'd been curious about her. He'd been drawn to her—maybe, he mused wryly, that was why he'd nearly hit her, in the Ensign regatta. Maybe he'd been unable to keep away. Certainly, increasingly that was the case.

Sam bit his lip. Did Valerie know, did she have any idea what she meant to him? Did she know he thought she was beautiful? That he believed she was brilliant? Did she know what she did to him?

The way she'd looked at him on the boat picnic on Sunday. The way she'd felt beneath his flattened palms, her bare skin like silk, like satin. The way she'd laughed and licked champagne from her lovely lips. The ride back, he'd had to hide the evidence of his arousal with a bunched up towel—not even the Atlantic was cold enough to calm him down, to quench his thirst, to stop the aching in his balls or to soften his straining cock.

And then, after such hard and heavy agony, the kind that couldn't be alleviated alone, by his hand and a bit of spit—the kind of agony that could only be alleviated by Valerie coming to him and confessing her mutual attraction, by her coming for him and sharing with him her own exquisite orgasm—after all the week's unalleviated agony, he didn't see her for over half a week.

Phebe Powers

At first he'd thought she'd been avoiding him. That he'd done something to scare her off. Or, more likely, piss her off. She'd been teaching, sure, but still. She had the evenings free. Why hadn't she stopped by? Why hadn't she said hi? They were staying on the same property. Sam's mind had gone dark and desperate. He'd felt a kind of burning sensation in his breast. But then Kat assured him that Valerie was always like this: busy, inaccessibly so, during the week as she balanced her summer job and her school-year prep; single-minded, race-oriented over the weekend, with the exception of the occasional outing—and even then, her cousins had to drag her out and she always brought a novel.

So, it wasn't Sam's fault. She hadn't been avoiding him, hadn't been staying away. But she hadn't sought him out, either. Hadn't made an effort to see him, or accidentally bump into him. She was like one of Abbottville's ghosts, except he rather thought a ghost was more likely to be his companion, to keep him company in the East Wing's ancient guest bedroom, than her.

But then just yesterday, after nearly a week's absence, she'd appeared at the door to the East Wing, demanding to see him. She'd taken him out on the Lasers, promised him some sailing practice—and sure, they'd ended up beaching the boats after an hour on the water, in order to strip and swim and fool around for a bit, including an almost-kiss that had left Sam wondering what she wanted from him, what the point was, beyond winning, of all this—but then they'd gone back to the beach, back to the boats, and spent the rest of the afternoon perfecting his beam reach.

When did Valerie ever take a break from sailing, other than to eat, sleep, or read? Would she have time for him later today, when the race was over? Would she even want to act on whatever it was between them? Or would she hold him there forever, in his constant state of arousal, like a phantom in the foreground of an old photograph, or a dragonfly in ancient amber?

The stopwatch ticked. Sam nodded. "Later."

"What's the time?"

"Ten seconds."

Wordlessly, Valerie steered *Girlfriend* below the committee boat, and for a moment Sam forgot his inner turmoil in favor of external terror—the fear that they'd collide with one of the many Herreshoffs clustered on the line. But he knew better than to doubt Valerie's sailing ability, whatever his concerns were regarding her attraction to him—he knew she felt it, he just didn't know if she felt it to the extent he did. So, he said nothing. He just watched, in amazement but not surprise, as Valerie maneuvered the sailboat between their nearest competitor and the big motorboat that was flying the Juniper Island Casino burgee.

They slipped right through the narrow gap, before Valerie headed up onto what she had called a close haul. Sam trimmed the jib sheet automatically. And suddenly, like the hull had been greased or an engine had been installed, they were off, escaping the crowded chaos of the fleet. Over the line—and not a second too soon.

"Did we make it?" Sam asked, slightly breathless. And why wouldn't he be? Valerie's confidence, her competence, her hard-won skill as a sailor could and should take his breath away. To say nothing of her windswept beauty, her grace and athleticism, and her steadfast determination. He wanted her to win. More than anything. Well, not more than he wanted her to—but those thoughts, those desires, those fantasies that set him on fire, they were selfish. Selfish and ill-timed.

Valerie nodded, a gleam of triumph lighting her dark eyes—like the North Star on a clear summer night. "But the start's only the beginning, Parsons. We've got a long race ahead."

The course seemed to stretch longer in practice than in theory; the upwind leg had felt interminable. Time would probably be passing more quickly if Valerie weren't so excruciating aware of Sam's proximity, of the strangely intoxicating scent of his deodorant and the soft, sweet sound of his even breathing. She could smell him despite the air's salt, hear him above the afternoon's breeze. She was keenly aware of him, right down to the pink shell of his ear, poking out from beneath her great uncle's hat, and the delicate golden hairs on the back of his neck.

He turned and she was lost momentarily in the light of his eyes and the way his lips always seemed ready to kick up into a smile. Good. He'd been too serious, before. She wasn't sure what was on his mind, but it had been unnerving to see him so… tense. "We're getting close to the mark," he announced.

Valerie nodded. "I have eyes."

His brow furrowed.

Shit. That had been too harsh. "Sorry, I—that was instinctive."

He seemed to consider this momentarily before smirking. "Your instinct is to be mean to me?"

Valerie rolled her eyes, but secretly she felt flustered. "I wasn't being mean. I was merely pointing out the fact that your observation was, well, obvious!" She wasn't handling this—whatever it was—very well. "But you're right. We are approaching the mark."

The rusted red nun was just two short tacks away.

"We've got a good lead," he continued, as though she'd never snapped at him.

"Yes. We had a strong start, and most of the fleet went too far out towards Sheep Island on the first reach. They lost time to the incoming tide and the lack of wind along the shore. What are you getting at?"

"Well," he mused, "the explanation was helpful. But I brought it up because I wanted to know what our strategy is."

Valerie huffed a laugh. "Parsons, you do exactly what I tell you. I'll take care of the strategy."

He sighed, apparently unsatisfied.

Lord, but she'd like to satisfy him. Off the water. Or on it. She could be creative.

"Harding, this would be a lot easier if you'd just trust me."

Biting her lip, Valerie avoided his gaze in favor of checking the stays. This immediately proved unnecessary, as they were perfectly taut and completely secure. She had a choice to make. And making it wasn't half as hard as she'd thought it would be. "Fine. I trust you."

He perked up immediately, just like the golden retriever he had to have been in a past life. Not that she believed in that sort of thing. "You do?"

Valerie sighed, but even as the breath left her body, she realized it wasn't a lie. "Yes. I trust you. Now pull in that sheet a fraction of an inch. The jib's luffing."

"Or maybe you're headed too far into the wind."

She stared at him in shock, but even her shock couldn't blind her to the fact that he was handsome. More than handsome. As well as impertinent. "Are *you* trying to tell *me* how to sail *my* boat?"

He chuckled, shaking his head. "No. I just enjoy getting a rise out of you."

Narrowing her eyes, Valerie reached for a sponge that was sitting in the bottom of the boat, forgotten amidst the rigging. He watched her with some confusion as she dipped it in the water, soaking it, and then—without warning—chucked it at his head.

The wet sponge hit him square in the face. Sam was silent for a moment, clearly shocked, and Valerie immediately regretted her immaturity. But then he started to laugh. "Oh, I deserved that." He shook his head, eyeing her with a wicked gleam. Until he had some kind of realization, it seemed. "Harding..."

"Yes, Parsons?"

"If you had enough room to throw a sponge at my face, without hitting me in the face with your hand or arm, you're not sitting far enough forward."

Valerie stared at him. He was right. Sam Parsons knew how to sail. Well, that might be stretching it. But he knew the basic physics. After a moment's stunned silence, she shifted a half foot up the bench.

Sam shook his head. "Not far enough, Harding." He patted the bench beside him. "Come closer."

Valerie swallowed, eyeing his exposed thigh. Lord, but he wore short shorts. And they revealed a distinct lack of a tan line. "But—"

"Am I wrong?" His eyes glittered like the water, catching a stray refracted ray.

She shook her head, struggling to speak. "No, but—" Then she glanced up at the water, at the mark. "Shit. Tacking!"

Valerie pushed the tiller away from her and they both ducked. Sam deftly transferred the sheets. They switched sides simultaneously. But just before Valerie could find her seat, Sam hooked his arm around her waist and tugged her toward him.

She gasped, and beneath her t-shirt her skin tingled in the wake of his wanted touch. "What are you—"

Sam grinned. "Proving my point."

Almost imperceptibly, they picked up speed. Valerie eyed Sam with begrudging respect, and no small amount of arousal. "Fine." She inhaled and regretted it instantly, because she couldn't just smell the sea. She was close enough to smell *him*. The shampoo in hair, the detergent on his clothes, the honest and true and unadulterated scent of his skin, beneath the deodorant, beneath everything. And he smelled *good*.

"What's wrong? You've been staring at me for—" he checked the stopwatch—"six seconds. Which is not that long, considering, but we do have to tack again, and soon."

Where had he come from? This knowledgable, competent sailor? This clever, keen-eyed crew? Who looked like a movie star from Hollywood's golden age, and smiled like they shared a secret? Who smelled like salt and spice and—sex. Fuck. She wanted him, every which way. How the hell was she supposed to finish this race?

Valerie cleared her throat in a valiant attempt to clear her mind. "Tacking in twenty," she announced. "And then we'll be around the mark. You know what comes next."

"The spinnaker," he murmured, suddenly gloomy again. She hated it. Valerie hated it when Sam wasn't smiling.

Nevertheless, she nodded. "The spinnaker," she agreed, and pushed the tiller away from her once more.

"Valerie, I don't think I can do this." Sam's voice was low, without a trace of a joke.

She continued to let out the mainsail on autopilot as she processed Sam's announcement, as well as his uncharacteristic use of her given name. "But—"

He turned to face her, the bag in his hands. He looked so serious, so solemn. "In fact, I can't do this."

"Sam, we've talked about this. We've practiced this. Again and again and again."

He shook his head. "I *won't* do this."

"But—why?" She could feel the anger begin to rise, but first the bewilderment.

Kneeling, he watched her for a long time. "Because you need to do this."

"What?"

"You're the spinnaker whisperer. It's what you're best at. It's what you were born to do."

She attempted to level him with a look but was certain she just came across confused. "Parsons, that's ridiculous."

"Maybe. But it's true. You love this. You're good at this. You're the best at this!" He set the bag down. "You said you trust me, right?"

"Yes, but—"

"No 'buts.'" Sam smiled. He smiled and it was like the sun had come out from behind a cloud. "You trust me."

Valerie forced herself to act normal, which in this instance meant rolling her eyes. "Yes. And?"

"Trust me with the tiller while you set the spinnaker."

She shook her head immediately. "Sam, that's not the plan!"

"Screw the plan! Sailing is about instinct! It's about taking risks, taking chances, and at the end of the day victory comes down to making the right decision."

She stared at him. "Who taught you that?"

"You did. Not in so many words, perhaps. But still. It's all you." He smiled again—softly, sweetly, and Valerie realized she couldn't refuse.

"Fine. But if you crash this boat—"

He laughed, free and loud and clear as a pealing bell. "I didn't crash the Laser, did I? Get your ass up here, Harding. We've got a race to win."

As Valerie passed the tiller to him, her fingers lingered beneath his. A spark seemed to jump between them. It wasn't just attraction, though. Determination. Desire—for each other, yes, undeniably, but also for victory.

"Steer straight for that lighthouse," she instructed him. "Don't deviate. And do not let us jibe."

Sam nodded. "Aye, aye, captain."

Valerie knelt and set to work on the lines.

When the spinnaker went up, a solid triangle of crimson cloth, her great uncle's conquering flag, it billowed and folded for one terrible moment—and then it filled. It was perfectly set, and it flew like it was made to.

Caught up in her own breathless exhilaration, Valerie glanced back at Sam, only to find him watching her with something beyond admiration warming his gaze. And then the line twitched beneath her fingertips and she was forced to wrench her eyes away.

They maintained their lead for the entire downwind leg. In the distance, far behind them, pink and blue and multi-color striped sails dotted the distant horizon. No one was stealing this victory from Sam and Valerie, not this time. When at last they crossed the line, and the committee boat blew the victor's horn, Valerie laughed for the sheer joy of it. And Sam laughed, too.

And then, on the same instinct that told her when to tack and how much to trim, Valerie found herself turning away from the spinnaker, turning to face Sam. Her crew. And then he was standing. And then she was crossing the two steps over the wooden slats toward him. And then they were in each others arms. And then—they were kissing. Like the world could end, and they wouldn't even care. Because it felt so right, this kiss. This first step toward forever.

Sam cradled her with both hands like she was something precious, and she wrapped her arms around his neck like she might never let him go. As usual, his lips were parted in irrepressible laughter, which only made her kiss him harder, as though, standing on her toes, she could somehow make him take this seriously. Because kissing, like the sex it sometimes led to, was serious. Wasn't it?

Valerie had always thought so, but now, faced with a man who laughed even as he grew hard—and Valerie could feel him, eager and elongating at a pace with her own dampening desire, burgeoning against the butterflies in her belly—well, to be honest, Valerie wasn't sure of anything anymore.

How could kissing be a solemn thing, besides, when one's partner was prone to laughter? And when his laughter, in turn, inspired hers? Maybe Valerie had been kissing the wrong men. All her life, she'd been choosing partners who matched her—serious, strong-willed, slightly severe. Maybe Valerie needed someone like Sam, someone who spun silken pleasure out of the mundane: mouths, lips, tongues.

Silken pleasure, indeed, but like none she'd ever known—because as seriously as he took her—and of that this most recent race, with Sam's insistence on her setting the spinnaker, had made her feel sure and secure—he nevertheless didn't take himself too seriously.

His kisses were honest and hopeful and, well, hot. But what made them (for lack of a less clichéd word) magical was Sam's sense of humor. And Valerie wondered, with an aching cunt, as she flexed her abs against his increasingly present and persistently insistent cock, whether his kissing was merely a prelude—whether this was how he made love.

Sincerely, sweetly, sensually—but not with merriment, not

without good humor. Good god, Valerie wanted Sam. Needed him, now.

She tightened her arms around his neck, the tips of her fingers tracing the taut muscle of his broad shoulders, of his strong back. And when she urged him down and pulled him closer, because that was what she needed—him, closer; him, inside of her—he went willingly, eagerly, with an enthusiasm to match her own. He did as he was told, like always, whether or not she used her words. He bent to her, his lips curved but never once leaving hers, like a flower bends to the sun.

Lord, but he made her feel like she was made of light, like she alone could give him l—life.

Sweeping aside the word over which her mind had momentarily stumbled, because it was too soon and she wasn't ready, or maybe in this moment she was but he couldn't possibly be, Valerie left her mind and took refuge in the riot of sensation that was her ready body. She was amused, and aroused, to observe that when he bent down to better kiss her his cock jumped like the needle of a compass in search of north. Like all the world was askew and only she was true.

Valerie arched into Sam, letting her mouth fall open, letting his questing tongue in. She was rewarded with a guttural groan from him, his earlier humor overpowered by outrageous hunger. He clutched her to him and set about plundering her as though he were a pirate, pursuing some sensual treasure. His hand fell to her ass, kneading and squeezing, until at last she surrendered to the gravity of his hips, to the desperate grip of his fingertips.

Someone hollered and Valerie vaguely recalled that the committee boat was anchored nearby. But she was too given over to the general sensual onslaught—too drunk on Sam's scent: his deodorant's spice and the tang of his sunscreen and salt from the ocean's undiscriminating spray; too undone by the sweet taste of his lips, mingled with the memory of the morning's spearmint toothpaste; too aroused by his unyielding and yet slightly submissive touch—she was too horny, quite honestly, to care who saw them and what they were doing. Valerie was too high on Sam's kiss to be embarrassed by her present bliss.

Another someone hooted and still Valerie clung to Sam, her eyes shut against the daylight in unseeing delight.

A third person yelled with no small degree of alarm, "Watch out!"

Reluctantly, Valerie opened her eyes, blinking in the sudden light. Undeterred, Sam dragged his open mouth down her jaw and over the soft, sensitive stretch of her neck. Valerie shivered. But then she saw Mr. Hays, the typically jolly commodore of the Juniper Island Casino, waving his hands. And she followed the path of his pointed finger, to a sight that sent her mind and body into a very different kind of uproar.

"Sam!" Valerie wrenched herself away from him, lunging for the tiller, which had fallen some time ago to port. "We're going to crash into that boat!"

She yanked the tiller starboard as the lobster boat in question blared its horn for what might have been the millionth time, such was her mind's disarray. A young lobsterman in faded orange overalls was standing on the side of the boat closest to *Girlfriend*, which Valerie had successfully steered into safe waters. Seemingly effortlessly, he hauled a teeming trap aboard, all while shouting, in a thick Downeast accent, "Watch where you're going, Massholes!"

"Sorry!" Sam called back without seeming to mean it, reaching for Valerie once more. Laughing, he turned to her, looking vaguely dazed. "How did he know where we were from?"

Valerie shrugged as Sam's arms came around her. "Most of the folks who summer on Juniper are from Massachusetts."

Sam nodded once before bundling her up in his arms for a breathless kiss. Then, grinning unabashedly, he adjusted the front of his shorts.

"Yeah, I don't think the old waistband trick is fooling anyone."

Chuckling, Sam glanced downward. "No? Well, I guess I just don't give a damn." And then he shoved a coiled line off the edge of the bench, sat down, and reeled a wordless Valerie into his lap. "Shall we?"

A quick glance under the sail revealed no more lobster boats lying in wait, so Valerie nodded. And then they were kissing again, harder and faster and with increasing desperation, until she lost lost all sense and let go of the tiller once more in favor of wrapping her arms around Sam's neck again. His neck, which was suspiciously overheated.

Valerie pulled back, despite Sam's attempts to keep kissing her. "Sam…"

He chuckled against her lips, but when she refused to resume their kiss he buried his head in her shoulder and sighed. "I know that tone. What have I done this time?"

"Did you forget to put sunblock on the back of your neck?" She peered at the exposed, and increasingly pink, skin.

Sam groaned, mumbling something that sounded suspiciously like "yes" into the curve of her clavicle.

Valerie sighed, holding him tight. The staccato twitch of his cock when she trailed the tips of her fingers down his spine did not escape her notice. "Sam…"

He peeked up at her, all wide-eyed innocence. Except that those eyes, so blue and oh so wide, couldn't hide his hunger for her. "…yes?"

"You're lucky you're a good kisser." And then, before he could respond with one of his heart-stopping grins, she caught his lips in a crushing kiss—and allowed him to make her forget all about the fact that he was an unrepentant, and utterly inept, idiot.

Chapter 10
Derigging

Moaning, Valerie gripped the half-folded sail tightly. Fortunately, the boom was in its cradle so she could steady herself against it as Sam's fingers crept up her thigh. "Sam..."

"I love the way you say my name," he murmured, shuffling closer, crowding her with his tall frame. His cock was hard as he nestled it between her cheeks.

Valerie arched back against him, struggling to think straight. "Sam..."

"Yeah, Valerie?" He was as breathless as she was, his chest pressed against her back. "What is it you want? What is it you *need*?"

You.

No, that wasn't right. Valerie opened her eyes and was blinded momentarily by the bright sunlight. She cleared her throat, even as she reached behind her to clutch Sam's thigh. "Sam, I need you to pass me the sail ties."

He groaned in disappointment rather than pleasure. That wasn't right, either. Sam's groans should all be sensual sounds, drawn out of unrestrained delight. Valerie frowned. Then, she had an idea. Smirking, she stroked one hand up and down Sam's left thigh, smoothing over the muscles there. He was so sculpted, so beautifully defined.

"Sam," she repeated, sternly. "Be a good crew and pass me the sail ties."

Grumbling, he stepped away from her to retrieve the ties from the small cabin at the bow. Valerie admired his ass, tight and generously curved, as he bent and began to fish around for them. After a moment, he stood and handed her a bundle of narrow strips of woven fabric.

"Thank you," she murmured, stifling a smile.

He pressed a swift kiss to the back of her neck, his hands coming to cradle her once more. "Anything for you, my captain." Then he squeezed her waist.

Valerie swatted his right hand playfully. "A good crew always does exactly what his skipper tells him to." She paused, tilting her head to allow him access to her neck. "You know, Sam?"

He nuzzled her. "Yes?"

The monosyllable, mumbled against her exposed neck, made her shiver.

"You're a good crew." Then she turned around to face him, gazing innocently up at him. "Aren't you?"

His eyes narrowed as he caught on to the game she was starting to play. He nodded, slowly, smiling. "I aim to please."

Valerie couldn't help her own grin. That was how it was with him now. It was like, when they'd kissed, he'd unlocked her somehow. Unlocked her good humor, her playfulness, her wicked little grins, even a new and exciting tendency to tease, a desire to toy with him—it was all part of her unquenchable arousal. Her raging attraction to him. Right now, everything she wanted, everything she did—it was all for him. And it was all possible because she trusted him.

He'd given her a gift, in earning her trust. And she wanted to give him something, too. Not because she was keeping count, or trying to break even, but because... Christ, Valerie didn't know. She just wanted to make him happy, as happy as he'd made her in the last hour.

She turned around again, presenting him with her back—and

backside. "Since you're such a good crew… You can grind against me while I finish folding the sail and securing the ties."

Sam hesitated. "Are you sure you don't want help?"

Valerie laughed. "I've done this a thousand times, so I'm far better at it than you. Faster, too. Just be a good crew and say 'thank you.'"

He breathed her in, answering on the exhale. "*Thank you.*" Then his hands found her waist again, and he took a step closer. And then another. He closed in on her, until his cock was where it had been, pushing into her shorts until they creased. Sliding his hands down her sides, slowly so that she shivered, he gently pried apart the two halves of her ass and allowed his cock to fall forward, nestling in the tight canyon between her cheeks.

Sam groaned. "Fuck, Valerie," he whispered into her windswept ponytail. "You feel so good."

Valerie hummed her approval and set to work, only slightly encumbered by Sam's urgently hard cock sliding ever so slowly up and down, in between her spread cheeks. She hadn't been boasting, before; she could fold this sail with her eyes closed. So, she did. Rocking back into Sam's embrace, letting her own moans mingle with his, she folded the sail on the boom—and not sloppily, either—securing each section with a tie. When she had mostly finished, having used all but two of the ties, she stopped. Sam noticed her stillness and, likewise, ceased to move.

"Valerie?"

"Yes, my crew?"

He pressed a kiss to her jawline, his hands roaming north until they found her breasts, hard-tipped and eager to be held. Sam cupped one in each of his large hands, letting his fingers spread, grazing her alert nipples. He didn't move for a moment, simply allowed them both to revel in the sensation of his long fingers skimming over her soft t-shirt, supporting her full breasts better than any sports bra. Then, when she thought she might die of yearning, he began to knead. Valerie whimpered, even as Sam whispered, "Aren't you going to finish folding the sail?"

She nodded, leaning back into his warm embrace—which made her feel weightless—and reveling in the press of his irrepressible erection—which made her feel like a goddess. Her own arousal was achingly obvious, as well. Between her legs, at the apex of her thighs, she was wet. So wet, she was literally dripping—spilling out the side of her soaked panties, an inch down the left side of her leg.

A sudden breeze wicked the sweat that had threatened to bead away from her temple and Valerie gulped down the salty air thankfully. "I've got a better idea," she managed, after a moment's strained but sensual silence. "I'm going to tie you up, instead."

Moaning, Sam squeezed her breasts in wordless response, suckling on her neck. He let his left hand drift down her torso, over her flat abdominal muscles and the slight curve of her hipbone. His fingers slid over the band of her athletic shorts, and Valerie spread her legs automatically, arched her back instinctively—giving him access and herself, pleasure.

Sam's fingers ghosted over her clitoris—caught behind layers of fabric and yet so sensitive to any contact, so desperate to feel the pad of his thumb, so needy and so ready to come, he might as well have been touching her freely.

He trailed lower still, his index finger following the inner curve of her upper thigh. And then he found the trickle of arousal, like honey heated to a lower viscosity. Valerie felt it before she heard it, the rumble of his laughter. And she blushed—not because she was embarrassed, but because her head was all in a rush, and she needed him—needed his touch.

"Sam..." she whined, desperately.

He smiled against her neck, against the very stretch of skin where she just knew he'd left his mark. Then he whispered, huskily, "Is this for me?"

She nodded, incapable of words, so intense was her arousal.

Sam followed the sticky trail up her leg, to the crease of her thigh.

He swept his fingers under her shorts and over the gusset of her panties, groaning at what he found. "You're so wet, Valerie. I can't believe it. I—"

She arched into him, turning as she moved, crushing her lips to his. He moaned as their mouths met, half in surprise, but wholly in pleasure. Valerie pulled away, her hands on his shoulders, the two forgotten sail ties between her fingers, panting. "Don't derail me, Parsons."

His brows knit in confusion. "What do you mean? I thought—"

She shook her head, summoning all her strength, and pressed one finger to his lips. "Shush. I told you, I want to tie you up. Is that—" She faltered for a moment, but recovered her confidence when she saw the hungry gleam in his eyes. "Is that something you'd be into?"

Sam nodded immediately. "Are you—Have you ever done this before?"

Valerie shook her head. "I've researched it, though." On lonely nights. "And I know a lot about knots."

He chuckled. "That's right. You promised to teach me."

"Consider this your first lesson," she murmured, leaning in to kiss him again. After a long and lingering minute, she pulled back. "Sit down."

Without hesitation, he did as he was told.

When he had settled on the bench, Valerie knelt before him. "Before we do this, I want you to come up with a word, any word, which, if you say it, means I have to stop. No matter what."

"A safe word, you mean?"

"Yes."

Sam nodded. "You're taking this quite seriously."

Valerie frowned at him. "Safety always comes first with me."

Smiling, he agreed. "As it should." Then his smile turned to a smirk. "Let's go with something nautical. I like a theme."

"What?"

"What's it you say, when you're on a collision course and you have right of way?"

Valerie stared at him. "Starboard?"

"Starboard it is!" He chuckled. "I mean, not right now. But that's my word. That's my safe word."

"Alright." Valerie let the sex and sultriness trickle back into her tone. "Now, be a good crew and give me your wrists."

He hesitated. "Wait. Are you sure you want to do this?"

"Why? Are you not?"

"No! I just…" He gestured to the surrounding fleet. "Anyone could see. Which, honestly, I think is hot. The idea of you, doing whatever it is you're about to do to me, out on the water where anyone could witness it? Very hot. But I don't know if that kind of performance, that kind of publicity, is something you're into."

Valerie smoothed the ties between her fingers, slanting a look that she hoped was seductive and mysterious up at him. "You don't know everything about me."

Sam grinned. "Yet."

She rolled her eyes. "Shut up, Parsons. And give me your hands."

Obediently, he extended his bare wrists. Valerie tied the two ties together with a square knot. Then she took the now lengthier stretch and wrapped it around Sam's wrists, leaving him some wiggle room, so that he'd be comfortable and to prevent chafing. Recalling the tutorials she'd seen online, and her own knowledge of knots, she brought the ends of the fabric together and tied a serviceable knot, not too tight—a slight variation on the sailor's bowline.

Admiring her handiwork for a moment, she then glanced up at Sam. His eyes were bright with arousal, and something else. Valerie bit her lip. "How does it feel?"

Sam tested the knot, moving his wrists as much as the ties allowed. "It's surprisingly comfortable," he said, honestly.

Valerie leveled him with a look. "A good crew has faith in his skipper."

Sam laughed. "Oh, I trust you. More than you trust me."

Yesterday, or even a couple of hours ago, that might have been true. But not anymore. Something had changed, out on the water.

Sam had earned her trust and in doing so he had apparently also opened the floodgates.

Valerie shook her head, cradling Sam's face between her hands. "You're an idiot, Parsons," she whispered. Then she kissed him, channeling all her feelings—all her longing, all her hope, all her yearning, all her trust, and above all, all her tenderness—into the kiss. Sam, meanwhile, menace that he was, managed to tweak her nipple.

Laughing, Valerie pulled away. "I thought you were going to be good."

Cheekily, he replied, "Oh, I'm *very* good." Then his eyes darkened and he smiled, wickedly. "Just untie me. You'll see."

Valerie shook her head, although she couldn't say she wasn't tempted. "No. First, I'm going to have my way with you. My very good, and not at all wicked, crew."

"I think you'll find I can be quite—"

Valerie raised her eyebrows. "A good crew knows when to shut the fuck up."

Sam could be a good crew. And by god, he wanted to be one, for Valerie. In reality as well as in whatever sexy game they were currently playing. He'd never really been praised during sex before. Not beyond the typical. He'd never really submitted to anyone, either. Given himself up to the game, to his partner; given up control.

Now, he was doing both. And it felt good. How did Valerie know that that's what he needed from her? That he craved it, both in his dick and deep in his soul, her praise and her poise and her power, extended over him like a tender caress, like the mercy of an empress, with her kisses that were also commands?

Sam didn't even know what Valerie was up to, although he had an inkling or two, but whatever she planned to do to him, he was in. Figuratively, literally, all of the above. He could be a good crew, for her. He wanted to be her best crew ever.

Valerie gazed at him for a long minute, surveying him from head to enclosed toe. "This," she said as she reached for the sun-and-salt-bleached hat, "has got to go." She tossed it to the ground, where it landed with a soft thud on the wooden slats. "That's better." And then she smiled—first with a sigh of sweet satisfaction, then baring her teeth with a huntress' hunger—and Sam's cock gave an involuntary twitch in response.

Valerie noticed the movement, her dark eyes darting down to his lap. Above his wrapped wrists, in the gap between his forearms, his dick strained against his shorts—it was caught in the thin athletic material, trapped. What's more, the tip was beginning to leak, staining his light gray shorts a darker hue. Valerie licked her lips as she looked down at him. And then, apparently addressing his cock, she smirked. "I'm sorry, but you'll just have to wait."

Her eyes darted up to meet his gaze, searching for something. Approval?

Sam nodded, giving her the go-ahead.

Valerie returned her eyes to his now throbbing cock, still hidden —but hardly. The dark stain of his precum had spread slightly. "A good skipper knows her way around the boat—or body, in this case. I'm afraid I've got some exploring to do, before I even get to you." Nevertheless, she extended her index finger and slowly traced a line from the base of his shaft to his leaking tip. Her eyes widened slightly, in—was that wonder? Her smile was beatific.

Sam felt like he had been blessed by a saint who specialized in sex: the patroness of the petite mort, a goddess to whom he would always give in. Because Sam was ready to come already. And yet he knew, with surety, that he wouldn't be coming anytime soon. Not if it were up to Valerie. And he'd ceded control to her long before they'd started this game of good crew and wicked skipper.

Valerie came out of her kneeling position and took a seat beside Sam on the wooden bench. "Let's see," she murmured. "Where shall I start?"

With a delicacy and precision that brought to mind her treatment of the sheets, she traced the bindings around his wrists, then brought her finger up his arm—slowly, excruciatingly. She seemed to savor what she found there, on his forearms: the lightly defined muscles, the tanned skin flecked with bleached-blond hairs. So much so that she bent to press her lips to his forearm, following the trail her fingers had first traced.

Sam shivered when she parted her lips and let her breath warm his sun-drenched skin.

Valerie dragged her lips along the line of his left arm, dropping kisses every couple of inches. When she met with his bicep, she bit down lightly, even as he flexed for her. "You're beautiful," she murmured, glancing up at him. "Did you know?"

Sam shook his head slightly, dazed. He felt beautiful, under her tender ministrations.

Valerie frowned when she encountered the sleeve of his t-shirt. "I suppose I should have taken that off before I tied you up," she muttered, more to herself than to him. She skimmed along the soft fabric until it ended and she found his bare neck.

Sam knew what was coming next. He couldn't help himself; when she sucked and licked and suckled, it—well, it tickled. He started to laugh until he was shaking with it, until she was laughing too.

"I'm sorry," he gasped. "I'm so sorry—"

She silenced him with a swift kiss. "Don't apologize. I love the sound of your laughter. Especially when I'm the reason for it."

Sam nodded and Valerie kissed him again, her tongue tangling with his even as her hands found their way into his hair, carding and pulling and no doubt disheveling it beyond repair. Gently, she grazed her open mouth, her bared teeth, along his jawline until she lit upon his ear.

In a sensual whisper, she asked, "And are you ticklish here?"

Sam shook his head slightly. "No, just a little sensitive."

"Mmmm." Valerie smiled against his cheek. "I see." Then her tongue darted out to trace the curve of his ear's shell, following it down until she took his lobe between her teeth—tenderly, tugging at it lightly.

Sam couldn't help, and didn't try to stop, the groan that arose in his throat.

Evidently, this pleased Valerie, because she nodded approvingly and whispered, "A good crew communicates with his skipper." Then she sat up a little straighter. "And you've been such a good crew."

God almighty, it was like she had a direct line to his cock. Her kisses, her caresses, her words of affirmation, they all went right to his dick until he was so hard he thought he could come without any intervention at all. He could, but he didn't want to. He wanted to come in her hand, her fingers wrapped around his shaft, her palm stimulating his frenulum, her thumb spreading precum over his swollen head until—

"Oh god."

"Sam?" Valerie pulled back immediately, her tone suddenly one of concern. "What's wrong?"

Sam opened his eyes and shook his head and chuckled, a little embarrassed. "Nothing's wrong. I promise."

She didn't seem convinced. "What just happened?"

"I, uh…" She'd said a good crew always communicated with his skipper. And he wanted to be a good crew for her, didn't he? Her best ever? "I was just thinking about you," he managed after a moment, "about all the things you could do to me, to my cock, and I—I almost came just thinking about it."

She didn't laugh, but he hadn't really expected her to. She wasn't like other people, his Valerie. Instead, she nodded slowly. "I see." Then she started to smile, a slow and sensual curve of her pink lips that left him harder than ever and a bit breathless. "Well, I'd better start paying attention to your cock, then. Since you're so close, and since you've been such a good crew."

Sam nodded, his eyes wide with desperation. He flexed his wrists, pulled at his restraints, but Valerie's knots held. And Sam was glad of it. He didn't know what to do with his hands, or himself, right now. Besides, there would be time to hold Valerie later. Time and time and time again, if he had any say. And for all their current, and highly erotic, imbalance of power, he knew with certainty that she would let him have an equal say.

Valerie lowered herself to her knees once more, easing herself onto the sailboat's slatted floor.

Sam frowned. "Is that comfortable?"

Valerie huffed a laugh. "It's not a mattress, but I doubt I'll be down here for hours."

She'd be down there for seconds, more likely. Sam was almost painfully ready.

Her lips twisted in a way that he had learned meant she was focusing very carefully on something—in this case, that something being Sam—Valerie reached up and hooked her fingers into the sides of his athletic shorts. Exerting herself slightly, she eased them down until his cock sprang free—a sight that made her smile—and then some more, tugging the shorts down until they pooled around his ankles.

"You're not wearing underwear," she observed with some surprise and even more excitement.

Sam shook his head, distracted by the cool breeze that caressed his cock, wicking the wet fluid from its tip. "The shorts are designed so that the wearer can—"

He lost all ability to speak as Valerie lifted his bound wrists, looped them around the back of her neck, and, kneeling, shuffled in between his spread legs in order to lick a wet line up along the length of his dick. Her tongue flat, she traced her finger's earlier path from the base, where his cock was nestled in neatly trimmed and dark gold hair, to the tip, which was swollen and soaking wet already.

She pressed a kiss to the very tip before parting her lips—and suddenly he was engulfed down to the root in her warm, wet mouth. He could *feel* the back of her throat, *feel* her constrict around him when she swallowed. His head thrown back, his eyes wide with a view of the cloudless summer sky, Sam groaned even as Valerie moaned, sending vibrations all along his shaft.

As she sucked, one of her hands slipped between his legs and her fingers—clever, careful, and just the slightest bit calloused—came to cup his aching sac. She was gentle with his balls—tugging lightly, stroking softly—and even more gentle with his sensitive perineum, which she played delicately as though the stretch of skin were an instrument, and their love-making were a song.

"Oh my god." Sam's neck fell back of its own accord, his eyes rolling back into his head. "*Valerie.*"

She moaned in response, letting the sound resonate down his cock and throughout his groin.

"Valerie, I'm going to come."

She nodded, sparing a glance up at him. Her eyes were wide and a little wet, and Sam wished his hands weren't tied, so that he could stroke her cheek and brush aside any tears.

"You've gotta pull away," he panted, through a pleasure so intense it was almost pain. "If you don't want me to come in your mouth—Valerie, I'm going to lose it any second now—"

But she just kept bobbing up and down, with greater determination than ever, sucking his aching tip and swirling her tongue around his shaft, flicking his frenulum and soothing the single vein that throbbed along the underside of his dick.

"Valerie, darling, I can't—I'm gonna—Valerie! Va—"

He came hard and hot and heavy, painting the inside of her mouth white with his pleasure. She swallowed several times before she pulled back, catching the remainder of his cum on her lips, which were parted in laughter, and her cheeks, pink with her own pleasure. The sight was almost enough to make him orgasm again, as if that were possible, as if he hadn't just unloaded every ounce of himself in and on and all over her.

Licking her lips clean, Valerie glanced up at him mischievously. "I guess I'd better let you go now." She set about swiftly untying his shaking wrists.

When he was free, Sam pulled her into his arms, not caring that he'd probably smeared cum on his t-shirt. Kissing her hard, he held her close, and when he finally broke away to take a breath he pressed his damp forehead against hers and whispered with a tremor born of true pleasure, "Never, darling. Never let me go."

Chapter 11
Widow's Woods

"Sam!"

At the sound of his name echoing across the still water, Sam reluctantly turned away from Valerie and glanced back over his shoulder and the bow of the rowboat. Will was standing on the dock, waving.

"Sam!" He was holding something small and rectangular in his hand.

Sam squinted, continuing to row. When he gave up and straightened his neck, focusing on his form, he found that Valerie had narrowed her eyes, too. Smiling, Sam set aside his own confusion and just took a moment to admire the lovely view.

Valerie blushed under his heated gaze, no doubt recalling the promise that he had made in the wake of his orgasm—to lavish her in pleasure, to inspire in her sensations as erotic, as explosive, as those through which she had guided him, just as soon as they were on dry land. After all, he didn't want her to be uncomfortable while he devoured her dripping cunt—and those wooden slats were no memory foam mattress.

"What is that?"

Startled out of his sensual reverie, Sam shrugged. She had a better view than he. "Not sure. Can you catch us, when we land?"

She nodded absently. "Of course."

"Thanks."

Valerie smiled at him. It was a simple thing, her smile. One corner of her mouth quirked, then lifted. The effect was lopsided and deeply lovely. Her lips—those lips that he had kissed, those lips that she had wrapped around his swollen dick—Christ, but he was going to get hard again, if he wasn't careful—those luscious lips of hers, they curved. Gently but generously, like a rainbow's inverse.

But rainbows were the consequence of rain. And they two had known no storm.

Sam turned his head again, slowing the rowboat as he guided it into place ahead of the motorboat with the green canvas awning —*Grasshopper*, wasn't it?

Valerie, meanwhile, caught hold of a cleat and stood, impressively steady on her feet, considering the latent wake of a lobster boat and the slope of the rowboat's hull. She took the painter in her hand and jumped deftly onto the dock, then knelt and began to secure the little dinghy with a knot.

"Kat says you took forever to derig." Will had lowered his hands, and Sam could see now that it was a cellphone in his hand. His cellphone, which he'd entrusted to Kat before the race. The screen was, for some reason, lit. "I wouldn't know, I wasn't keeping track. I was busy with the Ouija board."

Valerie straightened. "Still no sign of your girlfriend?"

Will shook his head. "Alas, Mary-Anne appears to have abandoned me."

Sam gestured toward the phone. "Is there some reason you've got my cell?"

Will's eyes widened. "Oh! Yes, that's why I came down here. Kat sent me."

"And?" Sam reached for the phone. Will handed it to him

gingerly, as though it were an irritant. "Why is the screen on? Who's—"

"Oh! Right. Your girlfriend's on the line."

Valerie's stomach dropped.

Later, she assumed, she would remember this moment with rage and resolution. But right now she felt nothing. No, not nothing. She felt sick, dizzy, faint. She even stumbled back a step. For the first time in her life—no, for the first time since that day, that awful day in the park when she was seventeen—she was unsteady on her feet.

Sam reached for her, automatically it seemed, as he wore the dazed expression of one waking from a dream. Wordlessly, she pushed his hands away. Those hands, they had held her. So tight, so close, she'd thought—she'd hoped—he would never let her go. Now, though...

Valerie stared up at Sam, whose eyes were wide like a deer's in headlights. But she wasn't the one who had blindsided him. He wasn't caught unawares, the unwitting victim. "You... have a girlfriend?"

He opened his mouth and then closed it again.

Valerie's eyes filled. She shoved past him, hard enough to make him stumble. She didn't even look back to see if he'd fallen; she just ran. Across the dock, up the ramp. Along the narrow pier, up the short set of stairs. Up the hill, diagonally across the lawn. She ran until she reached the woods. But before she could enter them, before she could be enveloped by them, before she could lose herself to their sap-scented embrace, someone caught hold of her wrist and tugged.

She knew those fingers, that hand. It was Sam. Besides, who else would have the audacity?

"Valerie!"

It hurt, how it hurt, when he said her name. "Let go of me."

He let go of her immediately. "Valerie, don't run away from me."

She took a step forward, into the woods.

"Valerie. Please!" His voice was plaintive, and full of pain. As though he was wounded party. As if she'd somehow hurt him. But his suffering was nothing, could be nothing compared to hers—to that of the other woman. "Just listen to me. Please."

Valerie inhaled, slowly. It hurt to breathe. Still, she allowed the sweet scent of the pine needles to fill her nostrils. She let herself be soothed by the summer evening breeze, whispering its way around and about the trees. When she spoke, her voice was loud and steady and clear. "Make it quick."

Sam exhaled. "I don't have a girlfriend."

Valerie shut her eyes. "Don't lie to me, Parsons."

"I'm not lying to you, Valerie." He reached for her again, but she pulled away. "Look at me, please."

Wordlessly, Valerie refused. She didn't want him to see the tears that threatened to spill.

"Fine. Don't look at me. But let me explain."

She nodded, once.

"I don't have a girlfriend. I think I hesitated because I was confused, or caught off guard by the look on your face—God almighty, Valerie, I can never forget it. It was like—I don't know, but I could feel my own heart breaking." Was that supposed to ease her pain? He took a heavy breath. "The point is, Will misspoke. Or maybe he forgot that Camilla and I broke up."

Anger flared. "Don't blame my cousin. He's not the one who—"

"Fine! Maybe I forgot to tell him. But I doubt it. Because it's been well over a month." When she said nothing, he continued. "I haven't even talked to her in weeks! She broke up with me, and I'm glad she did. Because I didn't love her. Not like—" He broke off, abruptly. "Valerie, please look at me."

She shook her head, blinking her tears back. "What about the cracks, Sam?"

"What?"

"That first day, when she was trying to convince me to take you on as crew—Kat said you don't let them show. But that doesn't mean they aren't there. That doesn't mean you don't have feelings for your ex-girlfriend, still. I mean, it was only a month ago..."

Sam groaned. "Valerie, I don't. I told you, I'm glad we broke up! And Kat's full of shit, you know that. She was probably just trying to get you to hate me a little less."

Valerie huffed a humorless laugh. "Well, it worked." All too well.

"Good. Because I don't want you to hate me. I want you to hear me out."

She sniffed. "What's there to hear?"

"I—Valerie, please." He sounded desperate, like he'd die if she didn't turn around. "Don't make me say this to your ponytail."

Rolling her eyes, Valerie turned to face him. "What, Sam? What the hell is so important that you have to say it to my face?"

He was silent for a moment, his eyes so blue it was like looking at the sky, his blond hair still sticking up in all the places her fingers had been. The reminder of their love-making was almost enough to make Valerie turn and run. But then she remembered that she was made of sterner stuff. She could listen to whatever it was that Sam wanted to say. She could survive this wretched afternoon. "What is it, Sam?"

He smiled, ever so slightly, the corners of his eyes crinkling. And suddenly Valerie knew, knew what he was going to say. But it was too late to stop him. It was too late to—

"I love you."

And that was when the dam broke, when Valerie's walls went down. A sob wracked her chest, and suddenly she gasped for breath.

"Valerie? What's wrong?" His eyes were wide with panic, confusion, pain. Hers couldn't have been the reaction for which he had aimed.

Blinded by fresh tears, she started to back away. "Leave me alone, Samuel Parsons."

"But Valerie—"

She stepped further into the woods, stumbling over a root. He reached for her to steady her, but she tore herself away. "I said, *leave me alone.*"

"Valerie, I just told you that I love you! Why are you running away?"

She shook her head. "I'm not running." She swallowed a sob. "I'm walking." She wiped at the rivers, the torrents of tears that ran down her cheeks. "I'm walking away." Just like she had that awful day, in the sunlit park in San Francisco.

Except, somehow, this was worse. Worse than finding her father in the arms of a woman who was not her mother. Worse than agonizing over the position her discovery had put her in, her newfound responsibility to do the right thing. Worse than finally telling her mother the sordid truth, only to learn that she had known of her husband's various infidelities for years and done nothing. Nothing but keep his secrets, and make excuse after excuse after excuse.

This was worse than that. Somehow. Worse than watching her perfect family fall to pieces and wondering whether, if she had just been better, gotten higher grades or put away the dishwasher without having to be told, would everything still have folded in on itself, like a poorly set spinnaker? Were her father's failures, and her mother's misery, somehow, in some way, her fault?

No. Valerie wouldn't go down that road again. She knew better than to blame herself. After all, she wasn't the tactician of her parents' marriage. She hadn't held that tiller, hadn't set that spinnaker. But this, her present suffering? This was on her. She was, as she had so often said to Sam, the skipper.

Valerie had let down her defenses. She had let Sam in. And then she had fallen in love with him. For the first time in her life, Valerie knew what it was to love and be loved. And it wasn't like reading about it in books. It wasn't easy, it wasn't painless, it wasn't perfect.

Nothing in life was perfect and the more perfect something seemed—like her parents' marriage!—the more likely it was to have a crack in the hull, or a kink in the line, or a tear in the sail.

The flip side of love was suffering. Sam hadn't cheated on her. Hadn't cheated on someone else with her. That was all well and dandy and fine. His protests, however honest, didn't offer Valerie any peace of mind. Because now she knew. She knew just how bad it would hurt, if he ever did what she'd thought he'd done. Or if she lost him in any way, any way at all. Valerie knew now how it felt for her heart to break. And she could say with greater confidence than she'd had even on that first day that taking Sam on as her crew had been a mistake.

She couldn't bear to love him because she couldn't bear to lose him. So, she wouldn't love him. And then she wouldn't be able lose him—or herself, to heartbreak.

Resolved, but no less miserable for her resolution, Valerie dragged herself deeper into Widow's Woods. Meanwhile, Sam did as he was told. He didn't even try to follow her.

Small mercies, she supposed.

Chapter 12
Stuck In Irons

"Alright, class. We'll explain the drills again once we're out on the water. You know your partners. Start rigging."

Valerie's students jumped up from their seats and made for the ramp that led to the 420 float. Still standing in front of the whiteboard, Valerie closed her eyes, just for a moment, and allowed herself to feel.

She felt dreadful. Like dying would be preferable. How could she have done this? How could she have let him in? Valerie couldn't, wouldn't answer that question. Instead, she closed up again. Better to feel nothing than everything.

"Are you going to tell me what's wrong?"

Valerie opened her eyes to find James frowning down at her. "Nothing's wrong," she replied, automatically. "You should be getting the keys to the—"

He held up his hand. Two sets of motorboat keys with plastic floaties dangled from his calloused fingers. "You're lying to me," he observed without affront. "Why?"

Valerie shook her head. "We're in the middle of a class, James. We can't have a heart to heart."

"Ah, so it is a matter of the heart."

She groaned. "James, leave me alone." Apparently that was all she had to say, these days. Leave me alone.

He shook his head. "Why won't you let me help you? After everything you did for me, reuniting me and Estie—"

"Not all loves are meant to be," she muttered, before she could think better of it.

He eyed her curiously.

"James, please?"

At that moment, Amelia appeared. Valerie could have hugged her, she was so glad of the interruption. "Valerie? Where are the extra plugs?"

James put his hand into his pocket and pulled out a few bits of black rubber. "Did you lose one?"

Amelia shrugged, taking one of the proffered plugs. "It might have been one of the beginner kids. David and I were about to put *Tactician* in the water when we noticed it was missing."

Sighing, Valerie inclined her head. She was exhausted. "I'll remind them to be more cognizant of their boats' parts tomorrow morning. Plugs aren't expensive, but nor are they good for the environment when they go overboard."

Amelia nodded. "Thanks, James. Valerie. See you on the water." Then she took her leave.

"See?" Valerie shot James, who had opened his mouth again, no doubt with an intent to pry into her personal life, a look. "We can't talk about this right now. We've got a class to teach."

"Fine." James bent to pick up an errant marker. He handed it to her. "But I'm here, Valerie. You aren't alone in this, whatever it is."

Valerie's fingers closed around the cool plastic of the marker's shell as she blinked back some stray tears. "Yeah, yeah. Go check on the committee boat's engine, or something."

"Sure thing, Valerie. Oh, and you might want to cover up that hickey."

∽

"Hurry up, slowpoke," Kat called down to Sam, who was wrestling with underbrush.

"You're missing the most amazing view," Will added from some height above.

Sam nodded, trudging up the unkempt trail. They were climbing —if one could call it that, given the lack of a substantial incline—up the rocky hill that the locals called The Sailor's Skull and the summer folk referred to as Juniper Ridge. Apparently, millions of years ago, the entire island—this hill included—had been deep underwater. And so, Kat and Will had assured him, Skull Ridge (their attempt at a compromise) was a site of great historical importance. Fossils and things.

Sam didn't particularly care, given his submerged state of mind, but he had hoped the short hike would offer a temporary respite from love's bite.

"You can see the mainland from up here," Will announced. "You don't even need these binoculars. Why'd we bother to bring them, Kat?"

Sam made it to the rocky top in time to see Kat pluck the binoculars from their perch around Will's neck. She held them up to her eyes, adjusting them slightly. "So we could spy."

That would have ordinarily earned her a laugh from Sam, but today he couldn't be bothered with humor. He just shook his head.

"What?" She offered the binoculars to him. "You don't want to know what the Woosters are having for lunch?"

Sam sighed. "I don't care, Kat."

"They could be cannibals!"

Will blanched. "You don't really think that—"

Kat groaned. "No, William, my sweet innocent. Although, Mrs. Wooster might well have eaten men alive, in her wicked youth. I'm just trying to get Sam out of this slump. I mean, seriously, what happened between you and Valerie?"

"I told you, Kat. I don't want to talk about it."

Kat narrowed her eyes at him. "You gave my cousin an enormous hickey, then Camilla called, then Valerie literally ran—ran, mind you—away. What the hell is going on between you two? And I know it's just the two of you, because Camilla is *clearly* over you. She told me she was just calling to confirm that you weren't coming to Brianna's wedding. Apparently you forgot to rescind your RSVP."

Sam ran a hand through his hair and instantly regretted it because it only reminded him of Valerie, and her quick and clever fingers. "She didn't run away from me," he muttered. "She walked."

Kat was watching him with uncharacteristic concern. "Ran, walked, flew. I'm still just trying to understand what happened between the two of you."

Sam let his face fall into his hands. "I don't know, Kat. Okay? It makes no sense to me, either."

Kat tapped a finger against her pursed lips. "I wonder if..."

Automatically, Sam perked up. "What?"

Kat frowned. "We never talk about it, and I wouldn't tell you without asking her first except that the two of you are clearly in love—"

"Kat..." Sam warned, his eyes narrowed.

She ignored him. "And, more importantly, something is getting in the way of that love—but..."

Will plucked a berry from a juniper bush. "Maybe it's to do with her parents."

"I've never met her parents. We've never talked about her parents. And if she's worried they'll disapprove—"

Kat waved a hand and fiddled thoughtfully with a knob on the binoculars. "Parents love you. Yes, yes, we are aware. But that's not what Will's talking about."

Sam sighed. "Elaborate?"

Kat shifted with uncharacteristic discomfort. "Valerie's father is maybe not the best guy."

"How so?"

Will tossed the juniper berry off the side of the rocky outcropping. "He conducted several extra-marital affairs."

"Ah." Sam was beginning to see where this was going. "And Valerie found out, presumably."

Kat grimaced. "I can't share the particulars—it's not my story to tell. But the divorce was messy, and her dad's side of the family treated her and her mother like hell. One of the many reasons why she's so much closer to us Abbotts." She smiled, tightly. "We're not perfect, but…"

"We love Valerie. And Aunt Linda."

"We look after our own." Kat offered Sam the binoculars. "Including you."

"Yeah." Will patted Sam on the back. "We love you, too."

Sam swallowed thickly. "And I, you. Both of you."

Kat's hand replaced Will's, with rather more force. "Now," she announced, cheerily, "if you point those binoculars at that grey house, there on the point," she guided his hand, "you should be able to see a rather rambunctious golden retriever."

Sam did as he was told, taking in the sights Juniper Island had to offer. But all the while, he was thinking about Valerie. What she'd been through, what he now knew. And the knowledge of her father's infidelity, as well as Kat's suggestion that there was more to that story, made him angry, where previously he'd been hurt. Not at Valerie, but at her father and his family. At the world that had conspired to leave her and her mother adrift—but not alone. After all, Valerie had the Abbotts. She had Kat and Will and even her great uncle. And, now, she had Sam.

Sam Parsons might have been lackadaisical in his last relationship, but this—what he felt for Valerie—was love. As sure as port was the opposite of starboard. Good lord, she even had him thinking in sailing terms.

Sam would fight for Valerie. He'd give her space, he'd give her time, he'd give her whatever she wanted or needed—but he wouldn't let her slip away, like the sun setting on a wasted day.

Phebe Powers

On Thursday, Valerie took the long way around getting back to the Cliff House. She'd been doing it all week, avoiding the East Wing like the plague. She knew she'd have to see him again. They were still racing together, after all. She wasn't about to let something as inconsequential as a broken heart get in the way of her winning the series.

As she entered the small living room, she tripped over a bunched up bit of carpet—love unbidden, or perhaps a lack of sleep, had made her clumsy—and as a result she bumped into the teetering pile of books on the driftwood coffee table. The tall stack swayed for a second before collapsing into a mess of splayed covers and bent pages, the well-worn paperbacks scattering between the table and the threadbare sofa.

"Fuck," she muttered, then sighed as she stooped to pick them all up. Valerie hadn't touched the pile in days. Not since Saturday. She hadn't been reading, lately. Probably because all of the books she owned were about love—which wasn't the problem so much as the fact that they all ended in Happily Ever Afters. For the first time in her life, Valerie had lost her faith in the HEA. In the romance novel's ability to overcome all obstacles, to solve all problems, to wave all worries away.

Or maybe she still had faith, but it was reserved for other people, living other lives. She wasn't going to sail off into the sunset with Sam. Not now that she knew how bad it would be, how much it would hurt, if she ever lost him.

Valerie understood that she wasn't some kind of side piece. That he didn't have a girlfriend on whom he could cheat. But she'd thought, for a moment, for a minute or more, however long it took for her to run from the dock to the woods, that the worst had happened. That she had been the other woman. That she had fallen for a man who was capable of carelessness, of callousness, of cruelty. She had believed, for however long, that that was Sam. And it had very nearly broken her.

After all, she'd only just come to understand that she loved him. She certainly hadn't told him yet. She hadn't even mentally articulated it. And then, to suddenly be swept into a storm of misery? To be lost at sea emotionally, to be shipwrecked by such a revelation, foundered on the jagged reef of such immense and incomprehensible suffering?

Valerie couldn't do it. She couldn't love him. She'd have to force herself to forget him, or at the very least her feelings for him. Because she couldn't live with the knowledge that she could, at any moment, break. Because of him. Because of her love for him. She couldn't take that risk—and love, she'd learned the hard way, was always a risk. It was followed, inevitably, by loss. Well, Valerie might as well save herself some time and suffering. Better to extricate herself now, than ever to feel the way she'd felt on the Abbottville dock again.

The screen door slammed behind Sam as he made his way out onto the East Wing's porch. "Sorry, sorry!" He winced. He'd been hoping to escape unnoticed.

"What was that?" Will called from within. "Sam? Was that you? Where are you going?"

"Oh, don't worry about him," Kat replied loudly from the kitchen. "With any luck, he's going to rendezvous with Valerie and the make up sex will heal both their broken hearts."

Sam grimaced. If only. He hadn't seen Valerie in days. She'd been avoiding him, clearly. And he'd done his fair share of staying away, respecting her clearly communicated boundaries.

Tonight, Sam was simply going stargazing. No lover's rendezvous for him. Valerie had made sure of that, with her quick-set boundaries like a barricade. Sam had no intention of storming them, however, of going back on his word to give her space. She needed time to process things—that, he understood. But he was nevertheless afraid... What if, once she'd had time, now that he was giving her space, she didn't come round? What if she didn't fight for their love?

Because he knew, with his newly awakened sailor's instinct, Sam knew, that she loved him, too. His declaration wouldn't have elicited such a reaction from her if she didn't. But the problem was, Valerie had been hurt before. And she was stubborn, down to her core. What if she decided, in her willful obstinance—a trait, for the record, that he loved in her—that their love wasn't worth fighting for?

Sam walked up the hill, away from the light that spilled from the East Wing's windows, and into the velvet dark. When he was satisfied that he was far enough from the house to have some privacy, he lay down on the lawn and let himself lapse into emotion—unbridled, because he had no audience for whom to perform put-togetherness.

As he stared up at the unblinking lights, at Vega and Venus and the Dog Star, his vision blurred and he felt tears well in his eyes. Sam inhaled the scent of the sea and the swaying pines and as he exhaled he began to cry.

Roughly five or maybe ten minutes later, his ducts were dry. But his heart still hurt, as he gazed up at the bright night sky. And then Sam heard the soft fall of someone's foot. He sighed. "Will, or Kat, whichever of you it is, please go away. I'm trying to wallow in my heartbreak."

He heard a sharp intake of breath. "You."

Sam sat up. He'd know that voice anywhere. "You!"

"What are you—never mind." Valerie started walking again. Walking away from Sam. Except, she wasn't. She was walking directly, if unwittingly, toward him.

"Oof!"

"Ouch!" Sam pulled back his hand, which she'd stepped on. Then he felt his lips curve of their own accord, in what could only be considered the ghost of a smile. "Now who's causing the collisions?"

He could practically hear her rolling her eyes. "Don't try to be funny, Parsons." She paused. "Have you—Are we still on for Saturday?"

"The series race?" He nodded. "I wouldn't miss it for the world." She might not fight for their love, but he would. He would fight for it, for her, for the faintest possibility of a future together. Sam wasn't giving up the series, much less the race for Valerie's heart—before she extinguished their love's light.

"Right. Well. See you then." Then she disappeared into the darkness.

Sam lay back on the grass and gazed at the Milky Way. "Goodnight." But she was already gone. And then, because it was the truth and because he could, and because even if she couldn't hear him, she still needed to hear them, Sam added three more words. "I love you."

Chapter 13
The Third Race

The weather suited the general mood. That was all Sam could think about as he got dressed on Saturday. Well, it was all he would allow himself to think about, lest he lose his nerve.

Emerging from his bedroom, he bumped into Kat, her arms full of what looked like lobstering gear. "What's all this?"

She shuffled the mass of waterproof material in her arms. "Foul weather gear."

Sam picked up a jacket—red, with white reflective stripes—and tried it on for size. It fit surprisingly well. "What's with the shiny bits?"

"In case you get lost in the fog and we need to find you, obviously." She rummaged through the pile and pulled out a pair of waders that matched the jacket. "These go under your lifejacket."

He held them up; they looked long enough. "Whose are they?"

"My first cousin, John. He's not on island right now, so you're fine to borrow them. Just try not to drown? Foul weather gear is *expensive*."

Sam nodded. "Got it."

She turned, carrying the rest of the gear in the direction of the kitchen. "And come try on Will's old sailing boots. They'll be far better than his Sperry's, in this weather."

It certainly was storming out. Sam eyed the wet window panes and the grey fog that had settled over the great lawn. "Are you sure it's safe to sail in this?"

Kat shrugged, pushing open the door to the kitchen. Sam was knocked back momentarily by the smell of freshly cooked bacon. "Well, you won't die—not with Valerie at the helm. She's super certified in water safety and that sort of thing." She tossed the pile of jackets onto a chair. "But you might be maimed."

"By the rain?" Sam's brow furrowed.

Kat laughed. "No, my sweet summer child. By Valerie."

Sighing, Sam helped himself to a piece of bacon from a nearby plate and bit into it. "We're fine, Kat." A blatant lie. But she didn't call him on it. She just nodded and stole the rest of his piece.

A half hour later, he met Valerie at the Abbottville dock. She looked every inch the professional sailor in short sailing boots, like the ones Kat had thrust upon him, and green and white foul weather gear. "You're wearing a lifejacket underneath that, right?"

"Hello to you, too."

She huffed impatiently. "Don't waste my time, Parsons. Are you or are you not wearing a lifejacket under my cousin's foul weather gear? Because if you're not—"

He unzipped the jacket, and her eyes followed his hands, lingering for a moment on his waist. Interesting. Sam puffed out his padded chest. "Lifejacket, see?"

She nodded. "Right. Well. Switch it so the jacket's underneath."

He did as he was told while she continued to speak.

"I've just been down at the Casino, checking out the course. I took a picture of it on my phone, if you wanted to take a look." She made the offer cautiously, but not contemptuously.

"Thanks." Sam stepped closer to her, careful not to crowd her as she pulled out her phone from the inner pocket of her coat. She smelled like rosemary and mint, and he couldn't help but close his eyes for a moment, and let the achingly familiar scent wash over him. Then he remembered himself. Opening his eyes, he found her watching him warily. "Sorry," he muttered. "I'm just... tired."

Her eyes narrowed. "Go have a cup of coffee."

"I'm fine, Valerie."

"We can't afford to have you falling asleep—"

Sam held up a hand. "Really, Valerie. I'm fine."

She gave him a once-over. "Right. Let's get rigging, then."

It wasn't pouring rain, but it was misting. Heavily. And when Valerie pulled up the wooden slats to check, they both saw that water had accumulated at the bottom of the boat. The pool was several inches deep already.

"I'll hoist the mainsail if you bail."

Sam nodded, taking the strange grey manual pump with its red handle and plastic, tube-like extension from Valerie.

"Try not to pump water back into the boat," she muttered, turning her attention to the sail ties.

Good god, the sail ties. Would Sam ever be able to look at one and not see, in his mind's eye, Valerie? Her ponytail messy, her lips wide and wet, her eyes dark with desire?

His cock, rather inappropriately, twitched.

Valerie eyed him suspiciously but said nothing as he finally got to work, sucking water from the bottom of the boat up through the pump and out through the extension over the side of the boat.

They worked in silence together, one bailing, one rigging the boat. Valerie's fingers were quick on the lines—and clever, he couldn't help but remember. She had caught her lower lip between her white teeth and Sam tried and failed not to recall the feel of them, grazing over the head of his cock. He had trusted her, to the extent that he'd let her tie him up on a boat in the middle of the thorofare. And she had trusted him, too, until Will's unfortunately phrased interruption.

Sam frowned. He understood why she'd reacted the way she had, at first. True, her reaction had been stronger than he'd expected, but that only spoke to the depths, he had assumed, of her affection. And

The Best Crew

Sam wasn't about to complain about Valerie feeling things too deeply, not when he felt so strongly about her himself.

"What are you staring at?"

You.

"Nothing." Sam set the bailer down, tucking it beneath the starboard bench. "Are we ready to let go of the mooring?"

Valerie nodded. "I'll take care of the mooring, if you'll fold the sail cover and stow it in the bow."

Sam did as he was told. He was always doing as he was told. Because, as he'd observed, what felt like an eternity ago, it felt right. He liked to listen to Valerie. He felt safe, and comfortable, and competent—and besides, he liked to make her happy. Sam wondered if he'd ever see her like that again—happy. Even if it wasn't because of him, he'd like to see it. Which was why they had to win. Whatever the weather, however strong the storm, Sam was determined to take this seriously and help Valerie to victory.

The little buoy landed in the water with a splash. "We're off!" Valerie climbed back into the boat, brushing up against Sam, who was on his knees cramming the sail cover into the tiny cabin. He glanced up at her just as she looked down at him, and they stayed like that for a long moment. Then Valerie seemed to remember herself.

She tore her eyes away, and started towards the tiller. "We're not flying the spinnaker today."

That startled Sam out of his reverie, in which he wasn't wearing this ridiculous outfit, and in which Valerie wasn't afraid to so much as touch him. "We're not? But that's why we won, last time. We have to fly it."

Valerie pursed her lips. "Parsons, you've been on a sailboat four times in your life. Trust me when I tell you that this makes sense. We can't fly a spinnaker because there's too much wind and conditions are somewhat dangerous. No one's flying a spinnaker. Race committee made an announcement advising against it."

But Sam was still hung up on her demand that she trust him. "I do trust you," he murmured. "And you used to trust me, too."

Her eyes met his once more. "What was that?"

"Nothing." He swallowed, unable to maintain eye contact with her for more than a few seconds. He'd been holding it in for so long now, but it hurt. Christ, it hurt. His head and his heart and his very soul seemed to have been shredded—by three little words. *Leave me alone.* They weren't the three he'd been hoping for, or, rather, four. Because he'd said the three, the big three: *I love you.*

He'd hoped, apparently foolishly, that she'd say those three, plus one more: *I love you, too.* But honestly, he'd have taken any number, any combination, so long as *don't* didn't feature among them. Then again, maybe it would have been easier if she'd just said what he hadn't even had time to be afraid of her saying: *I don't love you.* Maybe, if she'd just broken his heart cleanly, it would hurt less. And he would have less to wonder about, less to dream about, less to imagine.

"Parsons!"

He jerked back to reality. The reality in which she didn't love him, and didn't trust him, but did need him—as crew. Sam sighed. They would win this race. And then they would sit down someplace warm and talk about what had happened. "What's up, Harding?"

"Get your head out of the clouds."

"Well, it's a little hard to do that, considering the fact that we are currently in the middle of one." He gestured at the mist that surrounded them. "Are you sure it's safe to sail in this?"

"Don't be short with me." She adjusted her grip on the tiller, guiding them out of the fleet and toward the starting line, which Sam could scarcely see. "And don't doubt my abilities."

"I don't doubt your abilities, Valerie." Sam passed his free hand over his face. "I just worry that, you know, we may end up swimming home."

She blew a stray hair out of her eyes. "Which is why you should still be bailing. We're taking on water even as we speak." She gestured toward the bottom of the boat, which was not so full as it had been, but certainly not dry and empty.

Sam reached for the bailer, even as he took the jib sheet between his teeth.

"Not like that!" Valerie stared at him.

He spat out the line. "What?"

"You'll lose a tooth—or, worse, the jib will luff."

Sam laughed without humor. "Heaven forbid."

"Just hold it on top of—"

"I got it, Harding." Sam balanced the jib sheet in one hand, the pump's handle in the other, and the main tube between his knees.

"And don't lose that extension," she added, eying the grey tube that was snaking over the edge of the boat, out of which water was spraying. "If you do, the bailer will basically be useless. And we don't have a back up, unless you're interested in wringing out that sponge a thousand times over."

Half an hour later, according to the stopwatch he'd had to fish out of from under Will's lifejacket and John's coat, the rain was coming down in sheets. Sam had to shout, just to hear himself over the howling wind. "Are you sure we shouldn't turn back, like the others?"

Valerie nodded fiercely. "Don't second guess me, Parsons."

"I wasn't!" He wiped the water from his face, an icy mixture of rain and ocean spray. "I was just—"

"Tacking!" She yelled, thrusting the tiller away from her.

Sam ducked as he transferred the jib sheets. Meanwhile, the bailer, forgotten during the tack, came perilously close to falling out of the boat. Sam saw the pump tilt out of the corner of his eye and, securing the jib sheet under his foot, lunged for the extension, which had come loose and was dangling overboard.

"What are you—Sam!"

Valerie's scream was the last thing Sam heard, before he fell face first into what felt like cement. Everything went eerily silent. And cold. He was incredibly cold. Belatedly, Sam realized he'd gone overboard.

At last, after what felt like a fearsome struggle with Poseidon himself, his head came free of the frigid water. Sam gasped for breath. Thanking god and Kat for his lifejacket, whose buoyancy was being sorely tested by the heaviness of his foul weather gear, he managed to open his eyes—and immediately choked on water. His eyes stung with salt. His limbs felt heavy. His blood seemed to move more sluggishly. And Valerie—Valerie and *Girlfriend* were nowhere to be seen.

It all seemed to happen in slow motion. Sam, lunging for the bailer, slipping on the soaked slats, tumbling headfirst into the ocean. Valerie couldn't stop it. She couldn't stop him. He was gone. She had lost him.

After a second's silence, Valerie became aware of the sound of her own voice. It was hoarse, because she'd been screaming Sam's name. She let go of the mainsail and shoved the tiller away from her, forcing the boat into irons in the hopes that it would slow down and give her time to find Sam. The jib was already loose, flapping like one of hell's Furies.

Valerie turned around and surveyed the water behind her. She called out his name, again and again. Christ, but she couldn't lose him. Not when she hadn't even told him that she—she *loved* him. Valerie loved Sam, and he needed to know.

Thinking fast, past the fear and the fury and the feelings that threatened to overwhelm her, Valerie reached for the main halyard, lowering the sail halfway down the mast. She didn't want the full reach of the mainsail, not with the wind blowing however many knots —this was about precision, not power. Valerie took the tiller in one hand and the jib sheet in the other and turned the boat around.

Scanning the water for a red jacket with white reflectors, she continued to shout Sam's name. Faintly, over the howling wind, she heard something. Then she heard it again.

"Valerie!" Sam coughed, struggling to keep his head above water. "Valerie! Over here!"

The Best Crew

And then she saw him. A flash of red, behind a white capped wave. Blond hair, darkened by the water and plastered to his tanned face. He hadn't worn Uncle Willie's hat today. Or if he had, he'd lost it. But Valerie didn't give a damn. "Sam! I'm coming!"

The next minute was the longest of Valerie's life. She managed to maneuver the boat downwind. Silently, she thanked god she'd lowered the mainsail because the boat was trying hard to accelerate. When she was level with Sam, less than a yard away, she pulled the boat up hard, one hundred and eighty degrees, until it was once more facing into the wind, stuck in irons.

"Can you swim?"

He nodded, or at least she thought he did. "Valerie, I—"

"Tell me later, Parsons! Right now, I need you to swim toward me."

Dutifully, he started to kick his legs, arching his arms in an approximation of a front crawl. Slowly but surely, he fought against the current. Meanwhile, Valerie reached under the bench for the extra lifejacket, and stuck her hand down into the hold for a length of unused rope. Looping the rope around the lifejacket's neck, she secured it with her strongest knot. Then she stood and, aiming for Sam's general vicinity, tossed the lifejacket into the churning sea.

"Grab ahold of that!" She shouted, just as the lifejacket hit Sam squarely in the face. Wincing, she yelled an apology.

Through chattering teeth and over the crashing of the waves, Sam managed to return, "Nice arm!" Then he clutched the lifejacket to his chest and closed his eyes.

Valerie pulled hard on the line, reeling him in until he was able to grab ahold of the boat. "Do you have enough strength to pull yourself up?"

He hesitated. Valerie decided that was a "No." She secured the tiller, lest it drift and throw the boat out of irons. Bracing herself against the bench, she bent and offered Sam her hand. "Take it, quick!"

He did as he was told, grasping her wrist. Together, they dragged him up onto the side of the hull—and then he tumbled into the boat, landing on his back on the traitorous wooden slats.

"Oh my god." Valerie knelt beside him, cradling his head in her lap. "Sam, open your eyes!"

He groaned, coughing up a small piece of seaweed.

"Sam, please!" Valerie's voice had gone up several octaves and her tears were falling on Sam's face, mingling with the rain, but she wasn't ashamed of or embarrassed by her emotions. It only mattered that Sam was alright, that he was safe, that she hadn't lost him after all. He was breathing, wasn't he? She checked his pulse—steady. Unlike her own heartbeat. The words rushed out of her, like water from behind a dam.

"I'm sorry, Sam. Please, just open your eyes. That's an order, alright? I'm not begging you, damnit, I'm telling you! Please, Sam. I can't lose you. I thought I could—because I was scared and a fool—but I can't. I can't lose you. I can't because I love you! I should have told you a week ago, I know. I'm sorry. I was wrong and you were right and you can hold it over me for the rest of our lives so long as you open your eyes. Alright? Just open your goddamn—"

Because he was a good crew—no, because he was the best crew she'd ever had, and ever wanted to have—Sam did as he was told. His eyes were wide and blue as the sky. Well, the sky on a rather less cloudy day. He looked vaguely stunned and suddenly it occurred to Valerie that he might have hit his head on the way back into the boat. She started to feel for a wound.

"Christ, Parsons! You scared the living daylights out of me. How's your head? Did you hit it? Talk to me, Sam. Say something!"

His blue lips quirked. "You love me?"

Valerie rolled her eyes, sniffing. "Obviously. Now, tell me—did you hit your head? How do you feel? Can you count to—"

Her words were lost in his lips, as he pulled her down for an upside-down and incredibly salty kiss. Valerie immediately pulled back. "Sam! Would you please take this seriously? You almost drowned! And we have to make sure you're not concussed—"

It was his turn to roll his eyes. "Shut up and kiss me, Valerie."

Her jaw dropped. "Excuse me?"

He smirked up at her from where he lay in her lap. "You heard me."

Valerie's hands automatically settled on her hips. "I think you're forgetting who gives the orders around here."

Sam grinned up at her. "Impossible, when you haven't stopped giving them since you pulled me out of the water." He reached up and gently drew her head down. "Kiss me, Valerie. Please."

She closed her eyes, which were still watery, and inhaled his familiar—if slightly waterlogged—scent. "Since you asked nicely..."

And then they were kissing again, and everything was right with the world. Until they both jumped at the sound of a motorboat's nearby horn.

"What the hell was that?" Sam said, his lips marginally less blue.

Valerie glanced over the Herreshoff's varnished trim. "Race committee. You should really let them take you in."

Sam sighed, coughing again. "Fine, but only if you come with me."

"I've got to sail the boat back!"

Shivering, he eyed her warily. "So, you're not finishing the race?"

She shook her head. "No, not without you. And you're in no fit shape."

He barked a laugh. "Good, because that would be certifiably insane. And I'm fine, really."

"You nearly drowned!"

"I was wearing a lifejacket!"

"What if I hadn't found you?"

"I trust you."

She huffed. "Well, I won't say you shouldn't. I do happen to be certified in water safety."

Sam smiled and really his lips were, for all their kissing, an alarming shade of blue. "I am aware."

She tried and failed to fix him with a stern glare. And then she remembered something. "What were you trying to say, earlier? In the water?"

He laughed, his teeth only chattering a little bit. "I was going to say, I placed first at NESCACS my senior year, and I briefly held the record for men's freestyle at Tufts. Of course I can swim."

She rolled her eyes at him. "I meant, 'do you have enough strength to swim?' I wouldn't have taken you out on a boat in a storm—in sunlight, for that matter—if I thought you didn't know how to swim. But congratulations, I guess?"

Sam smiled up at her, coaxing her head back down again. "Thank you. And I know what you meant. I just enjoy teasing you."

She began to protest, but as soon as their lips met, she promptly forgot what she was protesting and why. Valerie almost didn't hear the shouts of the students on race committee over her own moans.

"Hey, lovebirds!" Valerie jerked her head up and found James watching her with one eyebrow raised in amusement. He held onto her boat with one hand, and the hood of his rain jacket with the other. "Would you like a tow?"

She nodded. "Thanks, and can you radio the committee boat and let them know that we're forfeiting the race?"

Sitting up with some effort, Sam sobered. "Are you sure?"

She stroked his cheek and found that it was wet with a combination of the rain, the ocean, and her tears. "I'll forfeit a race for you." She bit her lip. "But not the whole series."

Sam chuckled, shaking his head. "Don't worry, I'll be ready to race again by next Saturday."

"You should still visit the clinic," James interjected. "The doctor's in, and he'll want to check you for a concussion."

Chapter 14
The Island Clinic

"Valerie!" Sam hissed her name with no small amount of urgency.

She glanced over at the man she loved, the man who had very nearly died not an hour earlier. Well, maybe that was a bit dramatic. He had been wearing a lifejacket. "What is it, Parsons?" He was supposed to be sleeping.

"I'm bored."

She huffed a laugh. "You're whining."

"There's nothing to do here. They don't even have a television! What self-respecting hospital doesn't even have a single TV?"

Valerie rolled her eyes. "It's not a hospital, it's an island clinic with a staff of two. One of whom is on holiday while the other takes a smoke break. Besides, they don't have the budget for satellite, considering they don't charge their patients."

Sam gazed at her thoughtfully. "You know what this place needs?"

She shot him a skeptical look. "What?"

"A nurse."

"What?"

"You know, like a hot, sexy nurse."

Valerie's jaw dropped. "Excuse me!"

Sam frowned, looking her up and down. Then his eyes lit. "That's it!"

She pursed her lips. "What's it?"

"You should be the nurse!"

"Sam, I'm not trained in medicine."

He waved a hand. "It doesn't matter. We'll get you sorted with a tiara and a tight little outfit—"

She choked out a laugh. "A tiara? You think nurses are all princesses? Wow, the near-hypothermia really did a number on you."

He rolled his eyes. "Oh, you know what I mean. One of those sexy little headdresses. I don't know what to call them. They're not hats!"

"They're called caps, Sam. Caps."

He narrowed his eyes at her. "Are you sure?"

"Extremely."

Sam shrugged. "Well, it doesn't matter. We'll get you all dressed up and patients like me just won't know what hit 'em."

She laughed dryly. "And you're sure about this?"

"Valerie! You're a certifiable smoke show! And you're certified in water safety. That's sexy! You're sexy."

"I know I'm sexy. The water safety certification is the least of it. I just also know that I already have a job. Two, if you count my position as head racing instructor of the Juniper Island Casino. *And* I have no interest in swanning about in white latex."

Sam sighed. "And you're sure about this?"

"I was a sexy nurse for Halloween, sophomore year of college." Valerie closed her eyes and shuddered. "The chafing..."

Sam nodded sympathetically. But then his expression turned sly. "You don't... still have the costume, do you? Back in Boston, even?"

Valerie barked a laugh. "No!"

"Are you sure? It's not under your bed, or in a box somewhere?"

She stared at him. "Yes! And no!"

"Because *this*," he said, gesturing toward his groin, "is what imagining you in a tiny little nurse's outfit does to me. All tight, and short, and—Christ," he groaned, his eyes pleading with her, "the way your tits would spill over the low neckline when you bent to take my temperature, or whatever—" He closed his eyes. And then he opened them again. "Honestly, Valerie, with or without the costume, *this*," his cock visibly twitched, "is what you do to me."

Valerie bit her lip. And then she made a decision. Without further hesitation, Valerie got up, closed the door to the hallway, and then crossed the room to sit on the side of Sam's bed. "Tell me more," she demanded, somewhat imperiously.

Sam shook his head slowly. "Let me show you, darling, what it is you do to me."

Valerie hesitated, then nodded. "But we have to be quick! The doctor will be coming back in ten. Maybe fifteen, if we're lucky."

He frowned thoughtfully. "I don't know, it could be fun."

"What could?"

Sam waggled his eyebrows. "Getting caught."

Valerie felt a thrill at the very thought of it. But she managed to roll her eyes. "In your dreams, Parsons."

"Mmm," he agreed, lying back with his eyes closed. "In my dreams…"

Valerie coughed pointedly.

He opened his eyes in surprise. "Yes?"

"Aren't you going to show me?"

Sam played coy. "Show you what?"

Valerie glared at him.

He laughed. "Oh, alright. If you insist."

Sam took Valerie's hand, which was resting atop the blanket, her fingers curled over the edge of the cot, and brought it to his lips. She was relieved to discover that they were no longer cold, although doubtless he still tasted of the ocean. Sam set her hand down to rest over his hospital gown, atop his abdominals.

"Very impressive," she remarked, with a hint of snark, although the breathiness of her tone betrayed her arousal. It felt good to be so close to him, but she wanted to be closer still.

Sam laughed. "That was just a rest stop. I'm so weak, you know, what with almost drowning and all…"

She swatted at his shoulder. "Not funny!"

His lips curved but he nodded with understanding. Then he guided her hand under the thin blanket, placing it atop his growing erection.

Valerie inhaled sharply and squeezed her legs together, even as her fingers instinctively curved over the thin cloth of his hospital gown and around his hardening cock. How she'd missed him during their week apart, especially this particular part of him.

Sam groaned. "Now *that's* what I'm talking about."

She stared at him in confusion, slightly distracted by the delicate throb of his dick beneath her palm. "What?"

"Has anyone ever told you you have questionable bedside manner?"

She leveled him with a look. "Because I didn't immediately drop to my knees and repeat the events of last week?"

He gently thrust up into her hand. "No, darling. But I wouldn't be opposed…"

"Oh?"

Sam shrugged. "Well, it's not quite what I was imagining…"

Valerie bit her lip, instinctively tightening her grip. The gown was growing damp with precum. "What were you imagining?"

"Aside from the—" He broke off in a groan as she gently twisted her wrist.

Valerie suppressed a smirk. "You were saying?"

"Aside from the nurse's outfit?"

She nodded, stroking him through the gown. "Because that's off the table, for now." Valerie did not miss the way his eyes lit up when she added that last "for now." Smirking, she raised her eyebrows at him, daring him to voice his desires.

"God almighty, Valerie," he spoke on an exhale. "I just want to be inside of you."

Valerie closed her eyes, inhaling deeply. Then she opened her eyes again, looking down at him. "Do you have a condom?"

Sam's pout would have been comical, had she not also been aching with arousal. "No..."

"I mean," Valerie glanced around the white room. "It *is* a clinic. They *do* run the island school's sex-ed program. They must have condoms *some*where."

Sam perked up immediately. And then he shot her an amused look. "You're advocating stealing condoms from teenagers?"

Valerie shrugged. "They can't be half as horny as the two of us together."

Sam moaned and bit his fist. "The two of us together..."

Laughing, Valerie nodded and continued to caress his cock. "Exactly. Case in point. We need them more than they do."

Having ascertained that the doctor was taking a lengthy cigarette break, possibly one that involved calling his wife back on the mainland, Valerie spent several minutes snooping around the clinic in search of condoms. She found them almost immediately in the supply closet, in a box labeled, 'SEXUAL HEALTH.' Tearing three off the strip, she snuck back into Sam's room. The look he gave her upon her entry was wild and desperate.

"Tell me you found them."

She grinned, holding up the strip of foil packets.

"God, you're brilliant. I can't believe my girlfriend is a genius." Then he froze. "Can I call you that?"

She decided to tease him a bit. "What, a genius?"

He laughed, but quickly sobered. "No, my girlfriend. Is that—Are we there?"

She pretended to think about it. "I mean, we're in love."

Sam grinned. "Oh, are we?"

Valerie ignored him, except for the blush that stole across her cheeks. "But 'lover' is such an antiquated term... And I'd hate to re-introduce you to Mrs. Wooster and Mrs. Adams as my lover—they'd be scandalized, not to mention jealous, since they'd obviously comprehend the term's implications!"

Sam chuckled, patting the bed beside him. He'd evidently scooted over to make room for her, although it was still a single cot. "Nah, they'd love it. I bet they've been rooting for us the whole time we've been racing." Then his face fell, slightly. "Is that a no, then, to the girlfriend question?"

Valerie crossed her arms. "You can call me your girlfriend. But I'll still always consider you my crew, first and foremost."

He shook his head, smiling. "Aye, aye, captain. Now, get that gorgeous ass over here. Stat. This patient needs a little TLC."

She settled onto the bed beside him, level with his waist. Leaning over him, she supported herself on one hand and pressed a chaste yet tender kiss to his lips. "Like this?"

Sam arched off the bed, catching her in his arms. "No," he mumbled against her lips. "Like this." And then he proceeded to ravage her with ravenous kisses, scarcely allowing her a second here or there to come up for air.

Valerie reached down to caress him as he continued to harden. Impatience embodied, she shoved his hospital gown aside, fumbling for his sizable cock. "Are we sure," she nuzzled her boyfriend's neck, earning herself his irrepressible laughter, "that the regular condoms are going to fit?"

Sam snorted, the sound of which made Valerie giggle. "I'm not super-human, Valerie."

She dotted kisses down his jawline. "Mmm, well, at the risk of sounding hopelessly in love... You are to me."

His hands climbed the sides of her torso, coming to cradle her cheeks. "Darling, if anyone's a superhero here, it's you. You saved my life, back there."

Valerie met his gaze, which was sincere as she'd ever seen it. "Oh, Sam."

He huffed a laugh. "Don't get too sentimental on me, Harding. I still want to fuck you senseless."

She kissed him on the lips, with all the gentle sweetness in the world. "And you can, Parsons. In fact, I think its in the best interest of our partnership that you do."

He narrowed his eyes up at her. "What's that supposed to mean?"

She shrugged. "Just that if you don't, I'm finding another crew."

In one fell swoop, he flipped them both so that he was on top of her, caging her. "You wouldn't dare."

A little breathlessly, she retorted, "Fuck around and find out."

Sam shook his head, laughing. "I'd rather fuck you."

"So, what's stopping you?" She demanded.

"Nothing!" He bit his lip. "Maybe I'm just nervous."

She frowned. "About what?"

"That afternoon, on the boat—" He sighed. "That was the best orgasm I've ever had. And I want to make you feel as good, as godlike, as you made and continue to make me feel."

Valerie bit her lip. "Sam, I should tell you…"

"Yeah?"

"I come really easily."

His brows knit. "What?"

She laughed. "I can achieve orgasm through penetration alone. Or by clitoral stimulation. Or both. The point is, I lucked out. Massively. It's easy, for me."

He stared at her.

"I mean, it make take a little practice, but… Yeah, I'm not worried. And besides, I did bring my bullet vibe."

His eyes practically fell out of their sockets. "Here?!"

She struggled not to cackle, and couldn't quite manage to roll her eyes. "No, you beautiful little fool." She stroked his hair down into a semblance of sanity, then mussed it again. "I meant to Maine. I brought it up here for the summer." She chuckled at his immediate deflation. "We've got time, Sam. We've got time."

He nodded. "I know."

"But I wasn't joking, earlier. If you don't fuck me senseless in the next five minutes, I will actually fire you and find another crew."

He shuddered. "Yes, captain." And then he snapped his hips so that his dick slid along her covered cunt.

Valerie moaned. "Do that again."

"In a minute, darling."

"Don't you dare—" She broke off with a gasp as his hand found its way to her leggings' waistband. And then dipped beneath the elastic, then beneath the waistline of her panties to that slightly unkempt thatch of curly hair. "Oh, that feels good."

He began to massage her clitoris, circling and toying with the little nub.

"Oh, yes."

And then, when she started to arch up off the bed, he moved his clever fingers south, to slide along her soaking slit.

"Oh, god."

He stroked her slowly, gently, but with increasing intensity until she was as slick as the sea.

"Oh, *Sam*."

He caught her lips in a crushing kiss, even as he pushed one finger into her. And then another. Probing, exploring, stretching, and then when he finally added a third, thrusting.

"Sam, please!"

"You like that, darling?" He panted, his own arousal pushing into her hip. He ground against her. "Does that feel good?"

Valerie nodded. "But it's not enough."

Supporting himself on one elbow, Sam kept up a steady rhythm even as he asked, "What can I do to make it better?"

Valerie nibbled at his neck. "You can fuck me."

He laughed, then amped up the intensity. "Darling, I am fucking you."

She moaned, squirming beneath him. "With your dick. With your big, thick, throbbing dick."

Sam caught her lips in a punishing kiss. "Oh yeah?"

"Yeah," she panted, her eyes closed. "I want your cock inside of me. I want you to fuck me with it, hard."

Her boyfriend palmed her breast beneath her thick woolen sweater and sports bra. "God, I love you. You're so fucking sexy." He paused. "But can I taste you, first?"

"You can lick your fingers," she offered impatiently. "But right now I want you inside of me."

Groaning, Sam dragged his fingers from her dripping cunt. "Watch me, Valerie." Then, without breaking eye contact, he sucked each of his fingers dry, one by one by one. "You taste like heaven, darling. Heaven, and the sea."

She rolled her eyes. "You nearly drowned an hour ago; everything probably tastes like the sea."

"Excuse me for attempting some slightly more poetic dirty talk!"

Valerie laughed. "I liked it," she whispered, gazing up at him. "I just like contradicting you more."

Sam's jaw dropped. "That's my line!"

She smirked. "I know. And I'm holding it hostage until your dick is six inches deep in my cunt."

Sam said nothing, immediately setting to work removing her leggings and panties. He rolled them down but didn't remove them, in case she needed to get dressed quickly, instead leaving them loose but restrictive around her ankles. "I'm going to leave this gown on," he murmured. "In case the doctor comes back in."

"Good," she said with a grin. "It's sexy."

He shot her a skeptical look but Valerie wasn't lying. Everything Sam wore was sexy. Everything he did and said, too. Things were sexy because he was the one wearing them, or doing them, or saying them. But right now, Valerie needed silence. More than silence, she needed Sam's cock: hard and thick and long—as long as her favorite dildo, although rather less purple—and slightly curved, as though similarly designed to deliver greater pleasure. She needed him inside of her, like she needed water to drink or air to breathe. Like she needed the sun on her face and the wind at her back and her fingers curled round the mainsheet.

Except Sam was better than sailing—a thought, she worried, was sure to send her to Davy Jones' Locker. And yet, she didn't regret thinking it. But she wouldn't say it. Not right now. Sam's ego didn't need the boost.

He spread her legs with a longing glance, and Valerie had to laugh. "You'll get a taste," she murmured, rather enjoying withholding her cunt from his quick tongue—because she knew how much better it would be, for both of them, if she made him wait, made him work for it. "Right now, though, I need you to fuck me."

Sam nodded, a look of fierce determination passing over his face. "I'm going to fuck you," he muttered, lining himself up. "I'm going to fuck you so hard," he said, as he notched the head of his dick at the entrance to her pussy, "that you forget your own name." He eased himself in, and she let him in, and, Christ, but Valerie had never felt so good in her life. Sam gritted his teeth, groaning. "I'm going to fuck you so hard," he said, as he pushed deeper inside of her, "that you forget god's name, too."

Valerie gasped, and not because of his blasphemy.

"I'm going to fuck you so hard," Sam said, as he bottomed out, "that you forget everything and everyone except me and the part of me that's inside of you." Sam snapped his hips once, and Valerie's vision went white, and then Sam started to move.

She lasted maybe four minutes, and he was gone as soon as she started to flex and flutter around him, like a delicate vise designed to milk every last drop from him. Still inside of her, he collapsed on her chest, hot and sticky and wet. Panting, they lay there in silence for several long minutes. And then he pulled out and, clearly struggling, staggered across the room to dispose of the condom.

When he returned, she had pulled her panties back up and was squeezing into her leggings. Sam settled down on the bed alongside her, the bed that was barely big enough for one of them, let alone two. Valerie snuggled into the crook of his arm and sighed.

"Come here," he whispered, "my captain."

She pulled herself onto his chest. "Yes, crew?"

He smiled dreamily down at her. "I want another kiss."

She smirked. "Well, far be it from me to deny you."

After another long, luxurious minute, something occurred to her. Valerie broke the kiss, pulling away with a groan and a mumbled curse. "Christ, but you're killing my record, Parsons."

Sam blinked dazedly down at her. "What?"

She gazed up at him, feeling hopeful and helpless to her own happiness. "You have singlehandedly destroyed my winning streak. Before you came along, I couldn't be beat!"

He grinned, lacking the decency to at least look abashed. "But you love me."

She sighed, unable to suppress her smile. "But I love you." She arched to meet him, brushing her lips against his in a breathy kiss. "God only knows why."

Chapter 15
In the Mist

"I still can't believe you fell overboard during a storm," Kat said, shaking her head from where she stood at the foot of Sam's bed. "*Such* a drama queen."

Valerie watched with amusement as Sam opened his mouth to protest, but Will beat him to it. "You say that now," he countered his twin, "but you were white as a sheet when you first heard."

Kat huffed. "It was shocking news! Probably the most shocking thing to happen on island in years."

Valerie ran a hand tenderly through Sam's hair in a valiant but ultimately vain attempt to de-dishevel it. "Well, I don't know about that. Remember when Charlie Stockton was caught putting weights in the bottom of Mrs. Wooster's boat?"

Sam shifted in his seat atop the hospital bed to better stare at her. "*Who* did *what*?"

Valerie laughed at her boyfriend's ludicrous expression. "Much good it did him. In the end, she still won the regatta."

"And he got sent home to Connecticut," Kat added with a satisfied smile. "I do love a bit of sailing drama. It's a shame we didn't see you slip. We could have sent your parents a video of it!"

Sam leveled Kat with a look. "That's the last thing my parents need to see, thanks. My mother would have flown in from Needham and my father would have had a heart attack."

"But they could have met Valerie! I'm sure Carol is *dying* to meet her future daughter-in-law."

Sam flushed. "I haven't really told her about—"

Kat's jaw dropped. "You haven't told your mother that you're in *love*? What a terrible son."

Sam scratched the back of his neck, and glanced at Valerie apologetically. "I've been busy…"

Will nodded. "I'll say. And it's not like there's any reception on this island, besides."

Kat laughed. "We have wifi."

Valerie took pity on Sam, countering her cousin, "Yeah, and it's terrible. Besides, I've been running Sam into the ground—well, water—with this series business. Winners don't call their mother to talk girls when they could be out on the water running drills."

Her cousin raised her hands in defeat. "Alright, alright. I know when I've been beat. Sam, do you and Valerie want a ride back up to the compound? The doctor did say you could leave, didn't he?"

Sam nodded. "I'm good to go. But…" He glanced at Valerie, who raised a brow quizzically. "I'd rather walk."

Kat stared at her friend. "It's still raining!"

"It's drizzling," Will interjected. "I've always found a walk in the mist to be quite romantic. Is that why you don't want a ride?"

Sam looked at his hands, and something in his expression made Valerie's stomach do a little nervous flip. She steeled herself against the uncertainty. They had had their first fight, and survived it. Sam had survived a near-death experience, and Valerie had survived witnessing it. Whatever reason he had for wanting to walk home with her, whatever he wanted to talk to her about, and she rather thought she knew, she could survive. They could survive—together.

Valerie slid her hand into Sam's. He glanced up at her, surprise filling his bright blue eyes. "Something like that, I imagine," she replied to her cousin's lingering question.

Kat stood and pulled her rain jacket off the back of her chair. "Well, don't complain if you catch your deaths out in the rain! Come on, Will. We'd better head home and start mixing celebratory cocktails."

"What's the occasion?" Sam frowned in confusion.

Kat answered from the room's threshold, as she was already walking away. "Our favorite cousin's found someone who makes her happy."

Blushing, but not denying anything, Valerie leant into her boyfriend, pressing a kiss to his bare shoulder. "Come on, let's get you dressed in the clothes that my cousins brought, and then you can say whatever it is you wanted to say in the privacy of the road."

Main Street was empty of cars and a fine mist blurred the roadside, reducing the houses to phantom-like structures whose windows shone bright in the low light. They walked slowly, hand-in-hand, careful not to slip on the wet pavement or stumble where the asphalt gave way to muddy potholes.

Valerie swung her arm back slightly and Sam, not relinquishing her hand, mirrored the pensive movement. "So…"

He turned his head to look at her face, pale because of her diligent application of sunscreen, and framed by little dark wisps of hair that had escaped her braid and curled in the humidity—whether due to the present weather or their earlier activity. "So."

She bit her lip. "What is it you wanted to say to me, that you couldn't say to me in the car with my cousins?"

Sam nodded and tightened his fingers around her hand, drawing her a couple inches closer. "I think you know what it is I want to say, but because I value clarity over presumed clairvoyance… We need to talk about why you walked away. Not at first—that I understand—but after, when you knew I wasn't cheating on Camilla with you, when I told you that I loved you."

Valerie took her lip back between her teeth and began to worry it. After a long and somewhat tense silence, she sighed. "I think—I sometimes struggle with... love. The idea of it, and the messy reality."

"Because of your parents?"

Valerie glanced at him, her brow furrowed. "How did you know?"

Sam shrugged, adjusting his hold on her hand but not letting go. "Kat told me a little... But I'd rather hear it from you, in full."

Valerie grimaced. "Do I have to?"

Sam slowed, coming to a stop and turning to face Valerie fully. "Yes," he replied, searching her face for the confidence she'd seemed to have lost. He knew it couldn't have gone far, however. Valerie was strong, and brave, and generally brilliant. "I think you know we can't just fuck and say we've made up. If this relationship is going to go anywhere—and I want it to, Valerie, you know I do—we need to be honest with each other."

She nodded, her eyes closed. "I know, I wasn't being serious. Well, a little. It's not easy, Sam."

"I know." He took her other hand, drawing her close so that he could bend and touch his forehead to hers in a show of reassurance. "It hasn't been easy for me, either." Sam took a deep breath. "You hurt me, Valerie. When you rejected me, immediately after I told you that I loved you and minutes after I submitted to you in the most profound and pleasurable way possible."

She swallowed, her eyes open, wet and wide. But she didn't say anything. She let him continue.

"I thought I must have been a fool, to let you in like that. To let myself trust you, to fall in love like that. With someone who..." He trailed off, uncertain.

She twisted her lips. "With someone who?"

Sam exhaled. "With someone who could so easily, so readily break my heart."

Valerie shook her head immediately, fervently. "No! I wouldn't. I—"

"But you almost did. When you pushed me away, I thought... I wondered why. What I had done wrong."

"Nothing!" Valerie let go of his hands, raising her own to cradle his face. "You did nothing wrong."

Sam huffed a little laugh even as he closed his eyes and allowed himself to relax into her embrace. "I know that now, but... I still don't really understand." He opened his eyes and placed his palms over the backs of her hands. "Which is why we're here, standing in the rain in the middle of the road. We need to talk."

Valerie's eyes flickered as though she was resisting rolling them. "It's only a light mist, Parsons."

Her words drew out a little more of Sam's laughter. "Be that as it may, Harding..."

She nodded and let her hands fall from his face. "Come on, let's walk as we talk. That'll make it easier. And then we won't miss the sunset. It's always more beautiful after a storm."

Sam nodded and fell into step beside her, taking her hand once more. "I want to know what you were thinking. And feeling. I want to understand what was going on inside that beautiful head of yours."

Valerie huffed, shaking said head. "Flattery, eh? Well, if you must know... I was scared."

Sam cocked his head. "Why? Because I told you I loved you?"

She shook her head again, loosing several more strands from her braid. "Because I had realized that I loved you back. And I knew then, in that moment, after that terrible misunderstanding—I knew what it would be like to lose you, too. And I didn't think I could bear it. I knew I could not bear it."

Sam frowned. "I didn't think I couldn't bear to lose you, either. And, honestly, I don't know how I survived those few days without you."

Valerie bit her lip. "Me neither. I just sort of... went on autopilot. It was like my heart was breaking, and out of it was pouring all these feelings—nothing to do with you, either. But somehow, related."

"I still don't really understand," Sam confessed, rubbing his thumb over hers.

She looked up at him as they rounded a corner on the road. The entrance to Abbottville was close. "I think it does have to do with my parents. I don't know what Kat told you, but..." She took a deep breath and Sam squeezed her hand reassuringly. "My father is a heartless man. He cheated on my mother throughout my childhood. Again and again. In the end, I found out because I found him. In a park by the bay, kissing a woman who wasn't my mother. It all came out after that, like a torrent of unwanted truths. And I finally saw, I eventually understood, what my father's infidelities had done to my mother. How, in losing him, she had lost herself."

"And you were scared I would do the same to you?"

Valerie glanced up at Sam, her fingers tightly wound with his. "No. I know you would never. But... It was too much. I was too scared. I still am, by the way—scared. It's just that now I know what it is to almost lose you—not in love, but in life. You could have died in the middle of the thorofare. And, yeah, I did break. But what truly broke me was that I had already pushed you away. I couldn't bear to lose you, to a storm or to another person, but I really couldn't and still can't bear to lose you to my own stubborn fear and willful stupidity."

Even as she spoke, and the tears welled in her warm brown eyes, Sam drew Valerie into a tight embrace. "You're not stupid. And you're not going to lose me. Not to a storm, and not to another person. You have me. For as long as you want me."

She nodded into his shoulder, and he heard a muffled sob, as well as what he rather thought was another declaration of love. But, he thought, a mischievous smile curving his lips, it was better to be sure. "Sorry," he said, pulling away. "What was that last bit?"

Valerie sniffled and tried to snuggle back into his embrace. "I love you."

Sam shook his head and held her at arm's length. "Could you speak up?"

Valerie leveled him with a look. "I love you, Samuel Parsons," she announced, a bit louder.

Sam frowned and shrugged. "It's the strangest thing—must be the near-drowning. I really can't hear you."

She rolled her eyes, which were bright, if a little red-rimmed, and very nearly shouted, "I fucking love you, you inept idiot crew."

Sam laughed and laughed, and after a moment Valerie joined in, too. "Alright, alright… I love you, too."

Valerie huffed and shook her head and started walking briskly away, in the direction of the compound's driveway. "Come on. We'll be late for cocktails."

Sam caught up with her in two strides. "Ah, yes. We wouldn't want Kat and Will to drink all the G&Ts by themselves. Now *that* would be cause for a visit to the island clinic."

"Don't be silly," Valerie said as she deigned to let Sam to take her hand in his once more. "I'm confident we'll arrive to a tray of Dark & Stormy's."

"Oh? So, our drinks are determined by the weather?"

"Naturally."

Sam chuckled even as he shook his head, and allowed his girlfriend to lead him up the densely wooded drive.

Chapter 16
Summer's End

A week later, Sam was good as new. Better, because now he had Valerie.

They spent as much time together as they could, between her teaching and the work that had started to trickle into his inbox. On Monday, he made her breakfast before work, and greeted her after with a very public display of affection on the Casino dock. On Tuesday, he tried and failed to convince her to call in sick, and settled instead for treating her to homemade ice cream upon her return, after spending all day perfecting the recipe while Kat and Will worked.

On Wednesday, they woke at dawn and went for a run together, a run that ended in their making love on the shore of a secret cove. Either way, he'd said with a grin and a shrug, they'd gotten their exercise. On Thursday, they spent the evening sailing, because Valerie wanted Sam to practice steering while she set the spinnaker. And on Friday, Valerie's day off, the two of them took *Grasshopper* out for a boat picnic—Will and Kat stayed away, citing "sickening" amounts of PDA.

And then it was Saturday. Race day. As much as he wanted to beach *Girlfriend* on some far off island and make sweet love to his skipper beneath the late summer sun, Sam was eager to win the fourth and final series race—to show Valerie that he took her seriously, even when he couldn't stop thinking about the wet silk of her cunt like honey on his tongue or the little gasp she let out when he entered her—every time. Stifling a groan, Sam adjusted the suddenly constrictive front of his running shorts—although, he'd done more sailing in them than running, as of late.

"Are you alright?" Valerie eyed him curiously.

Sam grimaced as he willed his erection to go away. "Oh, don't worry about me. I'm only dying."

"That's not funny, Sam. You almost did—" As she surveyed him, her eyes caught upon his noticeably stiff cock. "Oh." She glanced up at his face, which he was sure was still contorted in a grimace. "Ohhhh." Then, her lips curved in a slow and knowing smirk. "Does it hurt?"

Sam wouldn't describe the ache in his balls as particularly *painful* but... if it meant another episode of Valerie playing nurse to his wounded soldier? "Desperately," he whispered, trying to look both sexy and pathetic.

Valerie pouted. "Poor darling. It's a shame I can't do anything about it until after we've won." She snapped back to business. "How much time until the start?"

Sighing, Sam checked the stopwatch. "Two minutes and twelve seconds." He supposed he shouldn't have expected any sympathy from Valerie. Not while she was getting into position for what she had called a "rabbit start."

After trimming the mainsail, Valerie turned her attention back to Sam. "You know, some sailors believe in kissing before the start—for good luck."

Sam raised one skeptical brow, even as his erection jumped at the idea. "Oh, really?"

Her eyes were dark and her smile had grown wicked. "Mmmm." She slid closer to him on the bench. "Maybe we should try it." She switched the mainsheet over to her other hand, the one that was already holding the tiller. "Just the once."

Sam nodded, mesmerized by her brown eyes—like dark chocolate, sweet but not without a kick of character. His lips parted in anticipation, he leaned closer to her to collect her good luck kiss.

Valerie shook her head. "Oh, darling. I didn't mean on the lips."

Sam's brows knit in confusion. "Then what—"

Suppressing a grin, she held a finger to his lips. "Keep an eye out for other boats," she whispered. "We wouldn't want to cause a collision."

Dutifully, Sam glanced around. There was no one nearby, although there were many boats in sight. "What are you—" And then he sucked in his breath. Because Valerie had bent, lowering her head to his lap, and was peeling back his shorts. Sam's cock sprang free.

"Oh, my. You are looking a bit swollen." She glanced up at him teasingly. "So thick. So long. So powerful." She looked back down at his dick, her breath ghosting over the tip in waves that made Sam shiver. "And all for me."

Gently, with excruciating tenderness, Valerie pressed her parted lips to Sam's throbbing tip in what was possibly the most erotic kiss he'd ever received. Then she drew back, pulling his shorts back into place. Sam hissed at the loss of her lips, and at his cock's sudden contact with the fabric of his shorts. He stared at her, wordlessly communicating all his longing, his loving, his need. "Valerie, please—"

She licked a pearly dash of precum from her lips. "A good crew is grateful for what he is given," she said primly, the statement paired with a positively evil smile. "Are you a good crew, Parsons?"

Sam groaned. "Yes, Harding."

She laughed. "Yes, I believe you're the best." Her smile faded, replaced by a twist of her lips that Sam recognized as the expression she wore when she was strategizing. A horn blew, signaling a minute until the start. "Perfect," she muttered. "We're perfectly in position. Parsons, trim that jib. Let's not waste the wind."

An hour later, they cruised across the line, Sam on the tiller and Valerie in the bow, her great uncle's bright red spinnaker flying like the colors of a conquering hero. As soon as the committee boat blew its horn, announcing their victory for all to hear, Sam let go of the tiller and lunged for Valerie, pulling her into a breathless kiss.

"Sam!"

He laughed. "Relax, Harding. There are no lobster boats this time."

She melted into his embrace. A minute later, however she came up for air, wearing an expression that didn't match Sam's mood.

"Hey, now. What's that face about? We won!"

She nodded solemnly, taking the tiller in hand. "Yeah, but we didn't win the series."

Sam frowned. "How do you know?"

"I did the math during the downwind leg. We've placed either second or third in the series, depending upon on how Mrs. Wooster does, as well as my coworker, James."

Sam sighed. "I'm sorry. I know how much you wanted to win."

Valerie shrugged, surprising him. "It stings. But there are more important things in life."

Sam laughed. "Like what?"

She gazed at him, and Sam nearly lost himself in the look in her eyes. "Like love," she replied. "Come on, let's derig. We've got a tea to attend."

"At the Casino?"

"No, at the old Adams Farm."

Sam frowned. "Mrs. Adams' place?"

Valerie nodded, steering them back to the mooring. "The Summer's End Tea. Her family hosts it annually." Then she perked up, seeing something or someone in the distance. "Look! It's my Uncle Willie!"

Sam glanced around, squinting across the bright waters of the thorofare. "He's with Mr. Wooster, right?"

"On the *Queen of Hearts*, Mr. Wooster's motorboat. He named it for his wife. Evil woman."

Chuckling, Sam shook his head. "You just don't like her because she's one of the few people on this island—possibly in the world—who can still beat you. She's perfectly nice to me!"

Valerie glowered at him. "She would be."

"What's that supposed to mean?"

"You're handsome, and polite, and tall, and good looking—"

"You're repeating yourself, my darling," Sam pointed out, but not without immense amusement. "So, are there lemon squares at this tea?"

Valerie nodded, her frown fading. "Oh, there's everything you could ever want. Lemon squares, ice cream, cookies, brownies, finger sandwiches, even cocktails. Especially cocktails. You'll see!"

Sam nodded, slowly. "Well, I suppose, if the refreshments are as such... And with Mrs. Wooster and Mrs. Adams to keep me company..."

She shot him an unamused look.

"I guess I won't need to bring the book you lent me!"

Mr. Hays cleared his throat. "And now for the Juniper Island August Series!"

Valerie and Sam sat on white Adirondack chairs on the front lawn of the Adams family's sprawling island estate. She held his hand tightly, finding herself full of nerves.

Sam leaned in to whisper, "Are you alright?"

Valerie nodded. "I think you should go up to collect the glasses, not me."

He looked surprised—touched, even—but then he shook his head. "No. Not without you."

"But, Sam, if it weren't for you—"

"Valerie. We don't have time to argue. Mr. Hays is about to say our names. Here's the deal: I couldn't have crewed an empty tea pot without you."

She rolled her eyes. "Don't be dramatic, Parsons. You're a fast learner and a good crew."

"Only because of you! You were the one teaching me; you were my skipper. Anyone else and I still wouldn't be able to tell my sheets from my cleats. You performed a goddamn miracle."

Valerie blushed. "Well... I still think you should be the one to accept the prize."

It was his turn to roll his eyes. "Only if you learn to accept a compliment, darling." He squeezed her hand. "Come on, we're doing this together."

A little ways down the lawn, in front of a table laden with prizes made of silver and glass—with the exception of a carved wooden heron that was perched atop a sturdy cigar box—Mr. Hays made the announcement. "In third place, against all odds and despite forfeiting a race, Miss Valerie Abbott Harding."

Sam pushed Valerie to her feet. She yanked him up beside her.

"Oh! And her crew, Mr. Samuel Parsons." Mr. Hays began to clap and the whole gathering, which must have been a hundred or more people, joined him in celebration of Sam and Valerie. Even her Uncle Willie, standing beside his nurse, was beaming with an air of recognition and pride. Valerie found herself getting slightly teary.

"Congratulations, you two," Mr. Hays smiled as he handed them each a whiskey glass into which a Herreshoff had been etched, flying the Juniper Island Casino's burgee. Below the intricate design, the year was written, as was the name of the series.

As they made their way back to their seats, Valerie shook her head. "I haven't placed third in years, not since I raced with Uncle Willie during his last year on the water."

Sam smiled at her, then squeezed her hand again. "Next year, we'll win."

Valerie grinned. "I'm holding you to that, Samuel Parsons."

"You can hold me to anything, Valerie Harding."

And that's when it hit her. The light streaming down on them, like the sky's blessing. The grass soft and green beneath their feet.

The breeze light but full of life. Sam was her true north, her safe harbor in life's storm. As long as she had him, she'd never be lost. And she'd never lose him, not truly, because you never truly lose the ones you love. The ones who love you, too.

"Hey, Sam?"

"Yeah?"

"Have you met my great uncle yet?"

Sam shook his head. "I'm afraid not. I've been so busy racing—my skipper's got me going like crazy—"

She swatted at him but he caught her hand in his, smirking. "Would you like to meet him?"

"Yes, but only if I'm allowed to kiss you, first." He drew her closer.

"Sam!" To her horror, she squeaked when he wrapped his arm around her. "We're in public!"

"That's never bothered you before..."

He had a good point. "Oh, alright. One kiss, Parsons."

He nodded, seriously. "Well, then. I'd better make it a good one."

One arm around her waist, one hand cupping her neck, he dipped her gently, then captured her lips in an all-consuming kiss. They carried on like that for a moment, in utter bliss, before Mr. Hays cleared his throat.

"As I was saying," the commodore continued, but not without a twinkle in his eye, "the first place prize in the Juniper Island August Series goes to—"

But Valerie couldn't hear him, because Sam had swept her off her feet and stolen yet another kiss—as well as the spotlight.

Straightening her blouse, Valerie giggled. "I think the winners won't be happy with us."

Sam, looking over her head at Mrs. Wooster and Mrs. Adams, winked at the two elderly women. Their frowns dissolved, and both their gazes took on a mischievous gleam. "Oh, I think they'll still like us just fine."

"You, maybe..." Valerie grumbled.

Sam chuckled. "My god, you really are jealous of two old ladies. For the last time, Valerie, you're the only one for me."

She sighed. "Come on, let's introduce you to Uncle Willie."

He happened to be only a few feet away from them, smiling merrily. "Hello, there!"

"Hi, Uncle Willie!" Valerie beamed. "I'm your great niece, Valerie."

"Of course you are," he said with a smile as welcome recognition flickered in his warm brown eyes—the same shape and color as hers, she'd been told time and again by her mother. "But who is this?"

Sam stepped forward, extending his hand. "Samuel Parsons, sir. It's an honor."

Uncle Willie shook Sam's hand, but he looked confused. "An honor?"

Sam nodded. "Valerie here says you taught her everything she knows about sailing." He smiled at her, weaving their fingers together. "Well, sir, she taught me everything I know. So, like I said, it's an honor to meet you." He lifted his prize, the lowball glass, and clinked it with the paper cup half full of lemonade that Uncle Willie was holding in one shaky hand.

"Tell me, son. Is she a spitfire, still, like she was when she was little?"

Sam chuckled as Valerie struggled to protest. "Yes, sir. And she's marvelous, too."

Uncle Willie nodded sagely. "Yes, that I knew." Then he sighed happily and took a delicate sip of his lemonade.

Tessa stepped forward, wearing a warm smile. "I'm afraid I have to steal your great uncle away," she informed Valerie apologetically. "It's been a long day. But if the two of you want to stop by the West Wing tomorrow, when things have calmed down a little, he should be full of energy. You might even convince him to go out on a brief boat picnic, so long as he stays on board and away from any unforgiving rock beaches."

Valerie nodded. "That would be great! What time should we come by?"

"Noon, or a little while after. He'll be up and at 'em by then." Tessa took the cup from Uncle Willie, who was starting to look a little tired. "Come on, captain, let's get you home." She smiled at Valerie, adding quietly, "I just wanted to make sure he was here to see you accept your prize. And to meet your new beau!"

Valerie felt her eyes fill. "That's so sweet of you." She took her great uncle's hand in hers and pressed a kiss to the back of it. "We'll see you tomorrow, Uncle Willie!"

"I certainly hope so, my dear."

Sam shook the old man's hand once more. "It's been a pleasure, sir."

A little bemused, but seemingly amused, Uncle Willie waved to them as he walked away, his hand on Tessa's arm.

"Right," Valerie said, surreptitiously wiping at her eyes. "Let's find Kat and Will."

Sam pressed a kiss to the top of her head. "No need." He gestured behind her. "They're here."

"Lovebirds!" Kat's smile was saccharine but her affection was sincere. "How's Granddad?"

"Good!" Valerie smiled brightly, sniffing. "We're going to go on a boat picnic with him tomorrow, if he's up for it."

Will patted Valerie on the back. "We'll join you! Kat can drive."

Valerie nodded. "Good plan. Are there any more lemon squares?"

Epilogue

"Are you really leaving already?"

Valerie nodded, offering her cousin an apologetic smile. "Sorry, Will. But I was grading papers all day—I really need an early night tonight."

"You're not even thirty, Valerie." Kat draped on arm over her cousin's shoulders, balancing a very full coupe glass in her other hand. "Don't stop living before you've even started."

"You don't need to worry about me," said Valerie, with an eye on her boyfriend, who was in the process of extracting himself from a lively conversation in the corner of the room, "I know how to have fun."

Kat smirked, following Valerie's gaze to light on her oldest friend as he approached the three of them. "Is that true, Sam? Have you been teaching our Valerie how to loosen up, how to live a little?"

Sam met Valerie's eyes, his gaze warm as a summer's afternoon. Mirth flickered in those pale blue pools, like sunlight dappling ocean waters. "Oh, no. Not at all."

"No?"

"No. You see, I'm the student in this relationship." He slid his arm around Valerie's waist and squeezed. "Valerie's the one teaching me."

Will scrunched his brow. "About what?"

"Life," Sam offered, his fingers toying with the hem of Valerie's sweater, slipping beneath it to caress her bare skin. "The universe. Everything."

Valerie pushed up off the ground to press a kiss to her boyfriend's clean-shaven cheek. He smelled good, like himself, and she caught a hint of his deodorant's familiar spice as she pulled away. "I don't know," she said, returning to Kat's earlier question. "I like to think that a skipper—this skipper, at least—has a lot to learn from her crew. However inept he may initially seem to be."

Sam chuckled, shaking his head at Valerie before turning to Kat and Will. "She still hasn't forgiven me for our first meeting."

Kat barked a laugh. "And why should she? You lost her a race."

"And with it, the whole regatta," Valerie corrected her cousin. "But you shouldn't be so quick to point fingers, Kathryn. You were on that boat, too. He wouldn't have taken the tiller had you not gotten bored of steering."

"What?!" Kat feigned outrage. "That's just not true."

Will, meanwhile, nodded sagely. "That is, if I recall correctly, exactly what transpired."

Kat turned to her twin and the two immediately started bickering.

Laughing, Valerie looked up at Sam. "Shall we?"

He nodded, smiling down at her. "Have you said all your goodbyes?"

"Yes, and you?"

He nodded again. "Let's get out of here." Giving her waist a squeeze, he guided her in the direction of the door. Sam grabbed their coats from the closet while Valerie waved at her cousins, who were too busy arguing to return the gesture.

Down on the street, under the light of a flickering lamp, Sam pulled Valerie in for a long, lingering kiss. "Yours or mine?"

Valerie didn't even have to think about it. "Yours is closer. And Raj did say he'd be out late, didn't he?"

Sam shrugged. "No, but he will be." His roommate, a friend from college, was a bit of a night owl. Still, he was always quiet when he came in, so it didn't really matter to Valerie and Sam. "You know, I meant what I said. I learn so much from you, all the time. And not just about sailing, or lesson plans, or the books on Brookline High's English curriculum. About how to live and, more importantly, how to love."

Valerie backed him up against the street lamp, whose soft glow fell lovingly on Sam's handsome face. "I meant what I said, too." She took his jacket's lapels between her fingers and held him there, against the metal pole, as she leaned in to kiss him with all the sweetness she could summon.

When they surfaced for air, a moment later, he murmured, "I love you, my impatient and somewhat irritable skipper."

Valerie smiled against his lips. "I love you, too, my inept crew."

He pulled her closer, still, until there was no space between their bodies and his heartbeat was indistinguishable from hers. "You know, they can probably all see us, down here on the street."

Valerie nuzzled the underside of Sam's jaw. "Who?"

He took a strand of hair that had come loose from her braid between his fingers and tucked it behind her ear as he murmured, "Oh, everyone at the party. Not to mention, Kat's downstairs neighbors. The whole street, really."

Valerie laughed. Then she pressed her lips to his neck, above the soft wool of his scarf, and sucked gently. "Let them look," she whispered against his skin, as Sam let slip a low moan of pleasure. "Let the whole world witness our love."

His hands found and cupped her ass, beneath the layers of her long coat and wool trousers. In one fell swoop, he scooped her up and spun her around until her back was against the pole. Breathlessly, she wrapped her legs around his waist. "Our love, but what about our love-making?"

The Best Crew

Valerie giggled. "I bet I can make you come without so much as touching your cock."

"Like this?" He thrust up into her, and she could feel his erection through the many layers of their clothing.

Valerie moaned and wrapped her arms around his neck. Stabilizing herself against the hard, cold pole, she ground against him. "Like this," she whispered in his ear, then nibbled at his lobe.

"You know I would never bet against you," he panted, thrusting again.

Valerie groaned, feeling herself grow damp with desire. "Why?" She tightened her legs' grip. "Because you love me?"

Sam chuckled. "No, because you're the kind of woman who always wins."

Valerie thought about this as she pressed kisses to the hard line of his jaw. "I suppose you're right. I like to win. In love, in fucking, in sailing."

"Exactly." He ground his cock against her covered cunt. "You're a winner."

"But so are you," she continued, between kisses. "Because you're my partner. My best-ever crew."

Acknowledgments

The Best Crew is a work of fiction and a labor of love. My second novella, it's just as important to me as *Après-Ski*, my first. And yet I almost didn't write it...

The idea for *The Best Crew* came to me belatedly. It was August and I was on vacation in Maine, on a small island that shall remain unnamed. I had finished drafting *Après-Ski* months earlier, and had yet to be struck with an idea for a sequel. Along with some friends and family, I had embarked on a boat picnic; we were watching a rather boring sailboat race. Boring, because we couldn't actually see the boats from our position on the curving shore. Not yet, anyway. Suddenly, however, a brilliantly colored sail—a spinnaker, if you remember—popped into view, pulling a lone and lovely Herreshoff into the lead. The sight was so mesmerizingly beautiful that I promptly lost my balance and fell off the paddle board on which I had been perched and into the icy water...

I started to write this book that very night.

The Best Crew benefitted greatly from the shrewd wisdom of my longtime editor, Jen, and I from her unwavering support. Moreover, more than a few typos and crimes of the comma variety were caught by my copyeditor's careful eye—thank you, Grace, for everything. I know how to sail, or at least I once did, but was never so skilled at spinnakers or starts, so my thanks as well to Nick and Pierre for their advice to an amateur.

As I said before, *The Best Crew* is a work of *fiction*. But for those of you readers who have been eagle-eyed enough to spy my borrowings from reality, thank you. If you know my real world well enough to recognize it in this fictional one, that means you've been a part of—played a part in—some of my happiest memories. As above, I wrote this book with nothing in my heart but love.

Finally, to riff on my epigraphic dedication: Pops, wherever you are now, you're the top.

About the Author

Phebe Powers cut her teeth on lithium carbonate tablets and historical romance novels. An avid romance reader as well as a firm believer in Happily Ever Afters, she's happiest when tucked away in the basement stacks of her local library, writing her own book or reading someone else's.

Also by Phebe Powers

If you enjoyed *The Best Crew*, check out the book that came before it: *Après-Ski: A Romance Novella* follows Valerie's Juniper Island coworker, James, as he meets and falls madly in love with his (not yet) girlfriend, Estie. If you like love at first sight, hot chocolate, and even hotter ski instructors, you'll love *Après-Ski*.

Après-Ski: A Romance Novella: Chapter One

"Seventeen bucks for a sandwich?" Estie stared at the sticker in disbelief.

"This *is* an airport," her younger brother pointed out, unhelpfully. "Didn't you get Mom's text last night?"

"Which text? There were rather more than several."

"The one where she told everyone in the family group chat to bring something to eat."

Estie eyed him skeptically. "Don't tell me *you* packed a meal."

Freddy shrugged. "No, but Ben made me breakfast before we left his apartment."

"At five in the morning?" She was impressed. Why didn't she have a boyfriend like that? Probably because she bolted at the first sign of commitment, typically.

Her brother smiled smugly, reading her mind. "Get your own soulmate. Or find a job that actually pays." As Estie struggled, due to the early hour and her lack of sleep, to come up with a suitably snarky response, Freddy picked out a bag of chips, two waters, and some spearmint gum. "See you at the gate!"

Estie sighed as her brother walked away. She loved writing, she really did. But... it was hard. Self-publishing took a lot of time and effort, the actual drafting and editing of her romance novels aside. And, as her brother had so kindly pointed out, it didn't quite pay the bills. Not fully. Thank god her parents were willing and able to cover a large part of the rent on her studio. Admittedly, the little apartment was a luxury, but she needed to be alone to write. Estie had tried and failed to have both a career and roommates. Then again, maybe she just had yet to find the right person to live with. Someone who'd inspire her to add to her backlist, not stall her creative process.

"Estie!"

She whipped her head around. "Oh! Hey, Miles." Her older sister's fiancé approached, wallet in hand. "Did you and Flo forget to eat breakfast, too?"

He shook his head. "Nah, but you know how she gets if she doesn't have two cups of coffee, and we only had time for one because the taxi arrived early."

"And they couldn't wait?"

"We were lucky to get a car at all. And I wouldn't put the love of my life through an early morning ride on the Red Line." Miles laughed, ever upbeat. "Anyway, do you want me to get that for you?"

Estie shook her head rapidly. "No, no. I mean, thank you. But no. I can afford a sandwich." A brazen lie, given the sandwich in question's price, but she had her pride.

"Fair enough." Miles knew better than to argue with her, especially at an early hour. "Besides, you'll be buying all of us sandwiches, when your next book becomes a bestseller!"

Oh, Miles. He really was sweet. "Sure thing." She smiled at him blearily. Maybe she needed a coffee, too... What time even was it? Estie checked her phone. A few minutes before eight, which meant it was almost time for her to take her meds. "Actually, Miles?"

He turned back to her. "Yeah?"

"Could you get me a coffee, too? Just a bit of milk, no sugar."

Miles nodded. "Whole or skim?"

"Whole." Estie believed in living fully, and that meant not settling for white water that called itself milk. "Thanks, M!"

"No worries." He smiled again, an absolute golden retriever of a man. "I'll bring it to the gate."

Estie grabbed the sandwich, budget be damned, and made her way to the self-checkout. There, she impulse-bought some dark chocolate, too. She'd save the sandwich for the plane—her thyroid medication required an empty stomach, she reasoned—but she could munch on the chocolate bar while waiting to board.

After a brisk walk back to the gate, Estie was greeted by her entire family, minus Miles: her mother, anxiously checking the delicate wristwatch that had once belonged to Estie's grandmother; her father, belatedly engrossed in Estie's second-to-most-recent release; her sister, snoring softly in her seat; and her brother and his boyfriend, who were engaged in a very public display of affection.

Estie felt nauseated—and lonely, as per usual. She averted her eyes, a touch dramatically. "Freddy, can you stop tonguing your boyfriend's tonsils for five seconds and move your bag off that otherwise open chair?"

Her brother disentangled himself from Ben in order to glare at her. "Find your own seat."

"There's nowhere else to sit!" She gestured around the waiting area. "They're all taken."

Grumbling, Freddy moved his bag. "Fine, but you're ruining the mood."

"I'm not sure there can be much of a 'mood' given that we're in an airport and it's eight in the morning."

Ben laughed. "Estie, you write romance novels. Surely you know that airports as a setting are romantic to the point of being a cliché?"

"Only if you're running through them, Ben."

"Whatever, Estie." Freddy rolled his eyes. "Consider any and all moods ruined by you, regardless."

Estie sighed. "Blame it on my *mood* disorder." Ben shifted uncomfortably, but Freddy was unfazed. He opened his mouth to argue, but Estie held up a staying hand as she slumped into the newly vacated seat. She was too tired to hear or herself summon a smart rejoinder. Where was Miles with her coffee?

"I'm going to try and get some writing done," she announced to everyone and no one. Then she pulled her laptop from its pink, padded sleeve. Prying it apart, she found that her word processor was already open, the waiting document as menacing as Moby Dick himself in its wordless whiteness.

When it came to writing, and life, too, Estie was a pantser, through and through. But for whatever reason, in the past month, the requisite words had refused to come. She was increasingly concerned —to the extent that she'd even considered going against the grain, throwing her lack of caution to the wind, and plotting out her next novel in advance of actually writing it. Like some kind of organized, methodical, sane writer. But the only two things Estie planned meticulously were falling in love and refilling her medications—which was why, her older sister had commented, a little unkindly, she did the latter monthly and the former never.

Estie sighed and started to type, trying to wrangle her muse as well as her mood. Method wasn't the reason for her block, but a lack of inspiration. And somehow she doubted she'd find any on this family ski holiday—the first in a decade, and her recently retired parents' treat... No, for her the slopes held only terror, and not romance.

While her siblings had significant experience on mountains all across America, as well as in Canada and even (in her sister's case) the French Alps, Estie hadn't skied since she was a kid. And that had been... an experience. Not only was she undoubtedly terrible now, at twenty-five she was old enough and wise enough to be terrified.

Still, Flo had promised Estie that she'd have fun in Blue Sky, the mountain town in Montana that lent its name to the nearby ski resort, that she would find things to do if skiing didn't work out, that she wouldn't be lonely or bored—even though her whole family would be abandoning her to the mild humiliation of ski school while they shot the chutes and dared the triple black diamonds. Freddy had been raving about something called the Big Couloir, only accessible by the very exclusive (and apparently expensive) tram. Estie thought it sounded dangerous, and that anyone who went up there willingly was deranged. Her siblings included.

But, Estie had for some godforsaken reason promised her family that she would at least try. And trying meant enrolling in the aforementioned ski school. For a day. After that, she'd stay home at the house they were renting and, keyboard in hand, continue to plead her case with the mercurial inhabitants of her mind's Mount Parnassus.

"Flight 362 to Boseman is now boarding at Gate 18."

Estie perked up, even as her sister jerked awake.

"Are we boarding? Where's Miles? We can't forget him again—"

Chuckling, Miles appeared at his fiancée's side, balancing three cups of coffee between his triangulated fingers. "Relax, sweetheart. I'm here. But I'm afraid we all might have to chug."

Estie took her coffee gratefully even as her sister tore the lid off her own cup and muttered, "Sophomore year trained me for this…"

"Alright, team. One more trip up the Magic Carpet, then I want to see your best pizza turns all the way down. Sound good?"

A chorus of small children cheered their approval. James had lucked out today—the kids were enthusiastic and quick learners, all of them. There had only been one tearful incident, and he'd quickly remedied that with a promise of hot chocolate and a sing-along when the day was done.

James didn't usually teach kids; he preferred working with adults. But his supervisor had given him a choice between work and no work, and he couldn't afford to take more than one day off a week, what with the pittance the resort paid him. Private lessons were the only real way to make a living on the slopes, and unfortunately James had yet to build up a substantial client list. Unlike his roommate,

Drew, who had a list of thirty or so clients so loyal that they'd followed him north when he left Vail for Blue Sky.

Still, James managed to make ends meet, supplementing his instructor's income with the occasional gig at one of the two bars in town. The locals might get tired of his Randy Travis covers, but the out-of-towners loved a late night rendition of "Deeper Than The Holler," and they tipped fairly well, once they'd had a few.

"Mr. James?" Kayla—who had informed him, immediately upon their introduction, that her seventh birthday was next week—tugged on the sleeve of his blue regulation ski jacket.

"Yes, Kayla?"

She gestured to her boot, which had somehow come free of its trappings. "My ski popped off."

"Do you remember how to put it back on?" James held her mittened hand so she wouldn't fall over as she balanced on one ski. There was nothing so detrimental to a student's confidence, or sense of safety, as a bad fall. Luckily, kids were pretty good at bouncing back. Better, in fact, than adults, who felt the humiliation more keenly with their grown up sensibility. It also helped that kids were shorter, which meant closer to the ground, so when they hit it, it didn't hurt so much. "Toe in first, yep, just like that. And then the heel. Stomp on it, like you're trying to kill a spider."

Kayla did as she was told, but when her boot had clicked back into place, her ski sliding a little against the packed snow, she looked up at James with eyes that were wide behind her pink-tinted goggles. "But spiders are good bugs. I don't wanna kill any spiders."

James considered this. "You're right, Kayla. I'll find a new analogy." Her nose wrinkled in clear confusion, an expression he recognized from having grown up babysitting his little cousins in Vermont; James realized he'd forgotten to adjust his vocabulary to better suit a seven year old. If she was still curious, he'd explain later. "Now, how about we join the rest of the group up on top of the slope?"

They were skiing within the confines of the designated teaching area, accessible to students and instructors only. There wasn't much to it, other than a small half-pipe where the students who were new to skis practiced the basics, and a short, not very steep slope called Lazy River. The teaching area also boasted the so-called Magic Carpet, which was really just a conveyor belt that carried skiers young and old up the miniature slope. There was another, bigger conveyor outside of the teaching area that led part of the way up a green, but James' students weren't ready for wide open spaces—or heavily trafficked areas—just yet.

Kayla inched onto the Magic Carpet, which was already whisking her peers up the hill, keeping her knees bent like they'd practiced. A few seconds later, it was James' turn. He squinted up the slope, counting helmets to make sure he hadn't forgotten a student, then shuffled onto the conveyor belt himself when he was satisfied that no child had been left behind.

At the top, the kids had spread out, hiking sideways across the ledge at the top of Lazy River. "Everybody ready?" James called out, throwing his voice so the kids could hear him above the whistling wind. They all nodded, some more dubiously than others, but generally they were a pretty fearless group. "Mike, why don't you show us how it's done? I want to see three wide turns and a nice slow stop at the bottom. No collisions."

An eight year old at the far end of the ledge saluted him. "Yes, sir!"

James saluted him right back. He'd be lying if he said he didn't enjoy the kids' respect, and how seriously they took this—unlike most people, including the majority of his family back east, who saw his seasonal gigs as well as his songwriting and singing as a couple of childhood hobbies that he'd wasted himself on, rather than budding careers to which he'd devoted the whole of his adult life. But who cared what they thought? They were estranged, after all, with the majority of them having cut him out after he'd taken his mother's side in her divorce. James sighed. Then he forced himself to do a little meditative breathing as he put the thought of his extended family aside and returned to admiring his students' gravity.

Après-Ski: A Romance Novella: Chapter One

Maybe he was rubbing off on them, after three hours of acquaintance. Drew, in amused agreement with pretty much all of the other instructors, did sometimes say James took himself and his job too seriously. But James wasn't a slacker, and skiing *was* serious business. It was dangerous, first of all, at every level. Second, and this was probably why he volunteered to teach Level One, bad habits were ingrained early. It was James' job to nip all that in the bud, and in its place to promote precision, proper techniques, and good practices—all leading to clean, crisp skiing. Safety first, and the skills would follow.

Mike took off, slowly at first, then picking up a bit of speed. He was one of the best in the group, although he tended towards hairpin turns. James monitored his wedge—the shape his skis made, their tips turned together—which was stable, and kept an eye on his tails—the back ends of his skis—as he finished his final turn, coming to a slow stop at the bottom of the slope, near the line for the conveyor. Mike's final turn had been a bit fast, and he'd yanked his upper leg into position, rather than shifting his weight and letting his edges guide him through a slower turn, but there was no use in yelling this information down the slope, only to have the wind whisk it away. So, James mentioned it to the rest of the kids and made a mental note to talk to Mike about it later.

One by one, the rest of James' students made their way down the slope under his close supervision, only one of them careening out of control—and, even then, Alexis managed to recover her balance before falling. Just when James thought she'd end up running into the mesh fencing that closed off the training area, she jerked her skis together and sideways at the same time, stopping so suddenly she looked a bit wobbly. James sped down the slope toward her. When he stopped, using the same maneuver she'd performed, albeit more expertly, his long skis sprayed her short legs with snow.

"Sorry about that," he said, gesturing to the white powder that was now spread across her shins. And then, more gently, "Are you alright?"

She nodded, looking a bit pale. "What was that?"

"What you just did? That's called a hockey stop. It's pretty advanced stuff. You don't play ice hockey, by any chance, do you?"

Alexis nodded again, understanding dawning. "A little, with my big sister on the pond in our backyard."

As he'd suspected. "That means you acted on instinct. Hockey stops are important because they can help prevent collisions, but they can also be scary because they happen really fast."

"I'm not scared!" She protested, straightening in her blue and green onesie.

James nodded gravely. "I'm glad to hear it. And I'm proud of you, you handled that really well." She beamed. "Now, shall we all ski over to the lodge?" The other kids had gathered in a cluster by the fence. "If we take it slow, avoid other skiers, and remember to stay in pizza mode, we won't have to worry about hockey stops." When working with kids, the instructors tended to use food-inspired terminology. Pizza was the name for the wedge shape beginners made with their tips, which helped them control their speed. French fries meant the more advanced, parallel skiing.

"If I stay in pizza can I have hot chocolate?"

James nodded solemnly at Sarah. "Of course." He always kept his promises.

An hour later, James sat in the instructors' lounge, which was really just a fancy name for the basement of the same building that housed daycare and the ski school office. The kids had all been picked up by their parents, some of whom remembered to tip, after a long round of Disney sing-alongs and a pitcher full of instant hot chocolate made with water—because the resort wouldn't spring for milk.

"Hey, man." Drew shuffled in, his gait smooth despite his clunky boots. "You done for the day?"

"No, I've got another round with the kids this afternoon. How was Sergio?" Sergio was one of Drew's private clients, one of the many who'd followed him from Vail.

"Good! We went up the tram—the line was long but, man, the

triple blacks were worth the wait." Only the most advanced skiers took the tram up to the top of the mountain, in pursuit of the triple black diamond trails and rocky chutes, as well as access to the Big Couloir.

"Was there enough snow?" Sometimes the resort had to close off access to the trickier trails, whose ski-ability depended on how much snow there was and the temperature at the top, as well as visibility. They generally wanted to avoid any rise in mortality rates, although the near-death nature of the experience didn't exactly deter the more fanatical thrill-seekers—quite the opposite. Adrenaline junkies, all of them. James understood that high, and the accompanying cravings, but he didn't seek it anymore. Not after his adolescence.

"Yeah, Thursday's storm replenished the snowpack. But I've been looking at the forecast and I'm not sure they won't have to close off some of the chutes, come midweek. It's going to be a scorcher. And you know what that means." Less snow, more rocks, ice in the morning and slush in the afternoon—typical spring skiing, made worse by climate change.

James frowned. "Still, spring break isn't over. The hordes continue to descend." He sighed. For a while there, after the winter holidays, there had been a lull in visitors to Blue Sky Resort. Weekends had remained busy, but the weeks themselves were fairly empty, leaving him plenty of time to write music and relax. The past couple of weeks, however, had seen the tranquil resort transformed into a zoo. It would be like this for the next few weeks, too. Until the end of the season, really, which was in April.

Spring break was the bane of James' existence as a ski instructor. It was worse than the winter holidays, in terms of visitors. Mostly because over Christmas and New Year's families found their way to the mountain, whereas spring break summoned not only families but packs of screaming college students who were more interested in the après, the after party, than in doing any actual skiing. They showed up in their "retro" onesies—garish recreations of '80s snow bunny styles—with their borrowed lift passes like fake IDs, not bothering with helmets and wearing ill-fitting rental skis. Little did they know, the Blue Sky après situation was mediocre at best, dire compared to exotic Courchevel or even the more local Jackson Hole.

James tried not to let his disdain for spring breakers get out of hand, but it was really frustrating when he was trying to take a group of beginners down a green only to find it clogged up by tipsy twenty-somethings. Personally, James didn't drink. He didn't do drugs at all, including caffeine—with the exception of a pot of perfectly brewed green tea, twice a day. Speaking of which...

"I'm making some tea, do you want any?"

Drew grimaced. "Not if it's that genmaicha stuff. Tastes like pond-water."

"To each his own." James bent to unbuckle his boots.

Drew sat and followed suit. "How were the kids?"

"Good, I had a good group." James eased one foot out of the tight fit, then the other, flexing his freed toes.

"You're back to adults tomorrow, right?"

James nodded, his mouth twisting into a line.

"You don't look too happy about it," Drew observed, taking in James' expression. "I thought you preferred working with adults."

"I do. I just worry."

"About?" Drew groaned as he got his left foot free, rolling out his ankle a few times.

"It's spring break. No one's going to take it seriously."

Drew laughed. "Dude, you've gotta lighten up. They pay you either way, so have some fun! You never know what's to come. Or who." He winked, and James rolled his eyes. Drew was convinced that James' latest dry spell was soon to end. James, on the other hand, had resigned himself to a lifetime of loneliness. At least, he thought, standing up, he had his music. And his tea.

Made in United States
Troutdale, OR
01/04/2024

16688735R00108